TIME OF BLOOD

TIME OF BLOOD

ROBIN JARVIS

With illustrations by the author

EGMONT

EGMONT

We bring stories to life

First published in Great Britain in 2017 by Egmont UK Limited
The Yellow Building, 1 Nicholas Road, London W11 4AN

Text and illustrations copyright © 2017 Robin Jarvis

The moral rights of the author/illustrator have been asserted

ISBN 978 1 4052 8025 9

61958/1

www.egmont.co.uk

A CIP catalogue record for this title is available from the British Library

Typeset by Avon DataSet Ltd, Bidford on Avon, Warwickshire
Printed and bound in Great Britain by the CPI Group

Stay safe online. Any website addresses listed in this book are correct at the
time of going to print. However, Egmont is not responsible for content hosted
by third parties. Please be aware that online content can be subject to change
and websites can contain content that is unsuitable for children. We advise
that all children are supervised when using the internet.

Take nae fright,
nor shiver wi'dread.
There's nowt to fear,
lest the Esk run red.

Whitby

West Cli[ff]

① Beach

② Khyber Pass

Pier Road

④

Hagerlyte

River Esk

1. Bathing Machines
2. Whalebone Arch
3. 199 Steps
4. Union Mill
5. Nannie's Cottage

St Ann's Staith

⑥

TIME-BURNED

In the shadow of the West Cliff, the fog lay thick over the broad sands, masking the margin between shore and sea. Its webbed fingers caressed the stone piers that reached out into the calm waters, coiling up around the lighthouses, absorbing the guiding beams from the great lamps and diffusing them in a wide milky spread before the harbour mouth.

The wooden bathing machines, which were stationed overnight at the foot of the cliff, appeared to float on the undulating mist like an armada of poky, white-washed sheds. On the beach before them, two small figures wended their way through the fog. One sported a broad-brimmed oilskin hat, the other a string of seashells about her brow; both wore ganseys of different designs. They were aufwaders – the half-forgotten fisherfolk of Whitby legend, who had dwelt on that coast long before humans settled there, but who now lived quietly and secretly in caves beneath the East Cliff.

Nettie Weever leaned against a large cartwheel of the end bathing machine and waited while her friend, Hesper Gull, caught up with her. Hesper was revelling in the fog, whisking and flailing her short arms through it, creating eddying waves. The deep wrinkles of Nettie's brow bunched together as she watched her friend's carefree play. Hesper had been so much happier these past few weeks – everyone in the tribe had noticed and the reason was known to all. Silas, her husband, was missing.

Silas Gull hadn't been seen for over a fortnight. He had always been prone to wandering off and spending time away from the caves on some sly venture, but he had never been absent this long. He was such an unpleasant, scowling and untrustworthy rogue, it was a relief not to encounter him in the tunnels and the other aufwaders understood why his mistreated wife was starting to feel her old self again. There were of

ARGUMENT
6d for a full half-hour

course those poisonous tongues who suggested Hesper had done away with her husband, but she was such a gentle creature that they weren't taken seriously.

Nettie almost hoped, for her friend's sake, that Silas had indeed suffered some fatal mishap. Hesper deserved better than that bullying villain for a husband and she wished she had done more to dissuade her from marrying him those many years ago. Silas had made her life wretched and, though he never struck her, no doubt fearing what her brother Abel would do to him, he crushed her spirit with more subtle cruelties. It was wonderful to see Hesper so cheerful and hear her laughter again.

Nettie lifted her wind-browned face to the night sky. Recently she had been reminded of those far-off days of Hesper's courtship by the sound of chilling cries, high above the humans' clifftop dwellings.

She started. There it was again, that horrible, unforgettable noise, like a wailing child. She had heard those mewling calls before, when a human magician called Melchior Pyke had stayed in Whitby, with his sinister manservant, Mister Dark. That servant had frightened the aufwaders; unlike most of the townsfolk, he possessed the gift of second sight and could see them. With a grimace, Nettie recalled how he prowled the midnight shore, often accompanied by a grotesque animal with bat-like wings. She gave a sorrow-filled sigh: that was also the time her human friend, Scaur Annie, had died.

She passed a hand over her face, grieved at the memory, then flinched when a gunshot echoed across the heavens.

'Deeps take me!' Hesper exclaimed, hitching up the cork lifebelt she wore over her gansey and joining Nettie by the bathing machine. 'Rowdy doings up there this night. That's the second of them stickbangers gone off – ear-achey loud they are. Why are them landfolk so fond of noise and riot?'

'I think that flying beast we've been hearing lately is being hunted,' Nettie guessed shrewdly. 'I hope they catch it.'

'There you go again. Can't be the same one you're thinking of, not after all this time. That's dead and done with and washed away.'

'I wish I could believe that. Much was left unexplained back then, and I am ill at ease. There is an evil abroad this night.'

Hesper shrugged. She took no interest in the affairs of humanfolk. The tribe was forbidden to have dealings with them. She was however fascinated by their bathing machines. When Nettie explained their function to her she fell about laughing. The idea that people would clamber inside via the back door, change secretly into different clothes, have the whole contraption pulled by a horse into the sea where those same people would emerge through the front door, step down into the water and immerse themselves, was the most absurd and overcomplicated ritual she'd ever heard.

Still, one thing was certain: Silas was not hiding inside one of them – they had checked.

Hesper resumed wafting her hands through the mist.

'When the time comes,' she said dreamily, 'it'll be on a night such as this that the moonkelp blooms.'

Nettie chuckled. 'I haven't heard you mention that old tale for many a year. It's good to hear you –'

Her voice stopped abruptly. Above the nearby stone pier there was a rumble like distant thunder. The air shook and the surrounding mist began to boil and curl. It was sucked up over the stonework, then swirled and twisted with mounting force to form a whorling vortex.

'Nine times bless me!' Hesper declared, holding on to her friend in alarm. 'What witchery is this?'

The coiling vapour stretched the length of the pier, becoming a wildly spinning tunnel that whipped and thrashed in every direction. At the furthest end, close to the lighthouse, a maelstrom of sparks and embers exploded into existence and roared through, igniting a pathway of purple fire. There was a dazzling blast of violet lightning and the uncanny corridor twisted faster and faster, branching with crackling, fiery veins.

'Look there!' Hesper cried. 'You see?'

Nettie could only nod in answer, her large sea-grey

eyes sparkling with reflections of that unearthly spectacle.

Within the tunnel a shape was forming. At first it was just an indistinct blur, but with every rapid pulse of light and peal of thunder it grew more solid and the aufwaders saw it was a human figure. Helplessly it tumbled forward, hurtling uncontrollably down the lashing tunnel, arms and legs dangling, head jolted from side to side. With dismay they realised it was little more than a child.

Punching through the seething fog, the figure went rolling on to the ground and lay there motionless. The blazing tunnel behind flared, and a blizzard of sizzling cinders whooshed over the pier. There was a snap of light, then all was dark and the vortex dissipated. The mist shrank back and the night was still once again.

Hesper slapped her face and rubbed her eyes.

'By the Three 'neath the waves!' she spluttered. 'What were that?'

Nettie did not know, but she pulled away from her, anxious to investigate.

'Leave it be!' Hesper hissed.

'They must be hurt!'

'But it's a maggoty landbreed!'

Nettie shook her head in disappointment. 'You sound just like Silas when you say words like that.'

Hurrying on to the pier, she ran to where the figure was sprawled on the ground.

At first Nettie thought it was a boy because of the trousers it wore – human females were always in skirts or dresses. But brushing the hair from its face she saw it was a girl, no older than twelve or thirteen. The unusual clothes were singed and smoking and the girl's skin was peppered with weird, glowing blisters.

Kneeling beside her, Nettie felt for a pulse. It was weak, but the stranger was alive. Then the aufwader made another discovery and she caught her breath in shock.

'Come away!' Hesper pleaded, having followed her. 'They're not our concern.'

'I can't leave her!'

'Esau would demand you do just that! You can't disobey the elder!'

'Esau isn't here and you're not going to tell him. She'll die if I don't help her! Besides, you should see this.'

Hesper approached reluctantly. She gazed down at the child's face and her kind heart pitied her.

'Here,' Nettie said, directing her friend's attention to something around the girl's neck. It was a string threaded with three ammonites. Hesper recognised them immediately and her mouth fell open.

'They belonged to Scaur Annie!' she cried. 'But how? We buried them with her.'

'I don't know, but I believe we just saw a doorway, and this poor child was flung through it.'

'A doorway to where?'

'Or *when*.'

'I don't like this. We shouldn't get caught up in it.'

'Too late wishing for that. Now, will you help me? We must bear this child to a place of safety where she can be healed, if healing is possible.'

'You're not thinking of smuggling her into our caves?'

'No.'

'Where then?'

'There is only one place. These snake stones are the sign of the Whitby witch; we must take the girl to her.'

Hesper frowned in puzzlement. 'But how do we know who that is?' she began, before the truth dawned on her. 'Oh, Nettie! You've been disobeying Esau all this time! You consort with these humans!'

'Only one of them. The witches of this town have never been our enemy. Help me carry this poor child to her door.'

'Me and you walk through them people streets? Have your wits leaked out your ears?'

'No one will see us two.'

'Just so! To prying eyes she'll look like she's floating, lighter than a fleck of sea foam! Nothing strange about that!'

'The fog will conceal her. I can't do this without you. Please.'

Hesper chewed her lip fearfully. She glanced over at the many huddled buildings of the human town and shook her head. Then she saw how earnest her friend was and she groaned with resignation.

'We'll rue this, I know it,' she muttered.

Between them, they gently lifted the unconscious girl and carried her from the pier. Even though the mist still clung to the town, Hesper's nerves were on edge and she looked about her constantly. When they crossed the bridge into the cramped lanes of the East Cliff, she was sure every dark window held a pair of hostile eyes and felt hopelessly vulnerable.

'How much further?' she whispered.

'Almost there,' Nettie answered. 'There's an opening yonder – through that and we're done.'

It was with great relief that they entered one of the many yards leading off Church Street and were able to lay the girl on the ground.

'Now, let's go!' Hesper urged, eyeing the cottages around them suspiciously.

'A moment more,' Nettie replied, removing the string of shells from around her brow and throwing them, one by one, against an upstairs window.

Hesper folded her arms impatiently.

'Who's that stood standing down there?' a stern voice called suddenly. 'If that's you, Eli Swales, I'll learn you to chuck stones at the casement of a respectable widowed lady's boudoir – I'll give you such a clout round the lughole you'll have to wear your hat backwards.'

The aufwaders stared up at the annoyed face leaning over the sill above.

'It's me,' Nettie answered. 'You must come down!'

All anger vanished from the voice and was replaced with an almost girlish excitement.

'Ooh, it's you, is it? And who's that there with you? Brought a friend? What must you think of me? I'll be down in two rattles of a sheep's whatsit.'

The face withdrew and moments later the front door opened.

'Fetch yourselves in – don't be shy. Why didn't you let me know in the usual way, or use the passage? If I'd known you was coming to visit I'd have spruced the place up a bit and flicked a duster about, and here I am with curling papers in my hair.'

'I'm not going in one of them stone boxes!' Hesper refused, stepping away.

'Don't be like that. I've got fruit cake keeping fresh in a tin. Happen you'll not have had fruit cake before. Ooh, you don't know what you've been missing.'

'Nannie Burdon,' Nettie greeted sombrely. 'See what we bring – a human child, spat out of the darkness. I fear there's only a gasp of life left in her.'

The woman on the doorstep peered through the mist at the girl lying on the ground.

'Get her inside,' she said sharply.

And so the Whitby witch and Nettie carried Lil Wilson into the cottage.

1

Grace Pickering placed the covered dish of curried mutton and rice on to a tray and shook her head.

'He won't touch none of it,' she said, wrinkling her nose at the aromatic scent that had filled the kitchen.

Mrs Paddock, the cook, leaned across the wide table and rapped the back of Grace's hand with a wooden spoon.

'The master's young ward is accustomed to stronger flavours than plain fish and mashed turnip, or whatever else you were used to in your shabby hovel on the East Cliff, my girl,' she scolded. 'They wolf down all manner of spiced dishes in foreign parts, them being foreigners.'

'He didn't fancy that kedgeree this morning, nor them devil's eggs at dinner time, if he even got so much as a whiff of them. I don't think Mrs Axmill is giving them to him. And my home weren't shabby –

just crowded was all. Kept it spick and span for my dad I did.'

'*Devilled* eggs,' Mrs Paddock corrected. 'And it was *luncheon*, you ought to know that by now, Flossy; you've been here since Penny Hedge day and here we are at the back end of August. And you just keep those nasty suspicions about Mrs Axmill to yourself. If you start flinging slanderous accusations around, you'll be out on your ear and worse.'

'Don't think I'd care much. It were a different household when I joined. It weren't on its ears back then. 'Sides, I can't never get used to being called Flossy!'

'That's what your name brooch says and that's who you'll be for as long as you're in service in this house so you can cut that backchat, else I'll put a dent in my turbot kettle the shape of your head. The mistress has her quaint fancies and she always likes her maids to be called Flossy. Goodness, you can't expect her to learn the name of every new chit of a girl what Oakeys her doorknobs and dusts her conversation pieces.'

'But Mistress in't here – and Esme kept her proper name. It's not fair. Flossy's what you'd call a dray horse.'

Mrs Paddock pursed her lips and the apron that barely contained her meaty frame inflated with indignation.

'Don't you mention that ungrateful wretch Esme Fuller to me!' she snorted. 'Up and vanishing in the dead of night, leaving me without a scullery maid to do the heavy work and wash the pots. I can only wish her the very worst and that's the Almighty's honest truth of it.'

'She were frightened, that's what it were – with good reason. She'd never have gone otherwise. It's ever since the family went away and *he* took over Bagdale.'

'Frightened? Fiddle-faddle! Mrs Axmill told me she'd slunk off with some gawky farm lout from the Dales. Disgraceful! Always knew the girl had dirty hands, but it's a stained reputation she's got now. Fie and shame! And her with a face covered in more blackheads than a Sunday seed cake. All I can say is they must be powerful short of female company up in them Dales if Esme Fuller is thought to be any sort of catch.'

'That's unkind, Mrs Paddock. I liked little Esme – and she worked her hands raw for you. There weren't a bone of a lie nor no wink of slyness in her whole body neither. She would've told me if she'd had a young man, and he'd have been the lucky one for it. Don't care what Mrs Axmill says. I don't trust her nohow; she's swanning about the hall like she owns the place nowadays. No, Esme ran off because of the goings-on here.'

'Plain absurdity! Why, there's less than half the work to do with the family gone and most of the rooms locked up.'

'It weren't the work.'

'What then, I ask you? It's clear as custard to me.'

'For one, there's that wild beast the new master keeps locked in the red bedroom. Why won't they tell us what it is? That great cage what got delivered was empty when it arrived but it in't now. I've heard the scritching and scratching and the rattling of the bars – and them weird cries it makes in the dead of night, like a tortured child in hell. Scared Esme half to death it did; she swore sometimes it were right outside her window – and she saw eyes looking in at her.'

'Through an attic window? It was in a hot-air balloon, I suppose, or perhaps it's a Barbary ape and clambered up the ivy? Head full of dreams, that useless juggins!'

'Weren't just that neither. It's the horrible feeling something is watching when there's no one about, things moving on their own. I'd heard about the ghost in this place before I come here, but didn't rightly believe in it. I does now and Esme said she'd felt foul breath on her face more than once.'

'Chestnut stuffing and nonsense.'

'And then there's *him*, the new master. There's a cruelness in his eyes – gives you gooseflesh it does. Devil's eggs would suit him. They say Old Nick is dangerous handsome and that's him right enough. I'm glad he's not at home tonight – wish he'd dine out all the time so I wouldn't have to serve him.'

'Oh, the scandal! And him a Most Honourable, a marquess – almost a prince where he comes from! How wicked to think such evil thoughts of your betters! You're only a squalid jet worker's daughter. I won't hear another word of it. Just you convey that there curried mutton to the new master's poorly ward before it gets any colder.'

Grace took up the tray and carried it to the door.

'Make sure you set it down in front of him yourself, mind,' the cook called after her, with a crinkle of concern in her voice. 'Then come straight down again. There's an apple dumpling in the oven which will surely get his appetite growling if the curry don't manage it.'

Grace caught the anxiety in the cook's tone. She wasn't alone in her suspicions then. Young Master Verne was as unlike his guardian as it was possible to be. He was a quiet, timid boy, whose thin face was marked with an expression of loss and grief. From the moment he arrived, Grace had felt sorry for him.

With a nod to Mrs Paddock, she left the kitchen.

Built in 1516, as well as being one of the oldest residences in Whitby, Bagdale Hall was also one of the finest. For many years it had fallen into disrepair, having been turned into a tenement, whose lodgers had chopped up the panelling and oak staircase to burn as fuel. Then in 1882 the dilapidated building had been acquired by Dr Henry Power, a renowned

London surgeon, who spent two years restoring and improving it.

Beneath the new roof, a hive of local craftsmen had replaced or installed almost everything: floors, plasterwork, magnificently carved fireplace surrounds, internal lighting, even the kitchen was a newly built extension with every modern appliance Mrs Paddock could wish for. The old hall had resumed its position as a grand dwelling once more and for six years Dr Power and his family had lived there happily, well liked and respected by everyone, including their servants. And then, unexpectedly, in that summer of 1890, the news spread rapidly about the town that the Powers had returned to London, and Bagdale had been let to a mysterious foreign nobleman, the Marquess Darqueller, and his ward.

Grace's shoes clicked smartly over the parquet floor of the entrance hall, which smelled agreeably of the turpentine, linseed oil and beeswax concoction she had polished it with yesterday. Passing a mirror, she paused briefly to check her appearance. She was more than presentable. Her face was clean and her auburn hair was neatly coiled beneath her white linen cap. At fifteen years old she was already a beauty and would bloom into even greater loveliness. Esme had called her an angel and had been in awe of her 'churchy' features, often joking she felt like a mucky potato next to a lily with sugar on. But Grace found her good looks an encumbrance; she was determined to make something of herself and paid no heed to the unwanted attentions of the ironmonger's apprentice or the grocer's boy, who both lived in hope that 'the jammiest bit of jam in all Whitby' would step out with them on one of her rare afternoons off. A childhood friend of hers, over on the East Cliff, spoke of nothing else but the wedding she planned to have one day. Grace wanted more from this life than that.

Ascending the impressive staircase to the first landing, she put the tray on a small side table and was about to tap on the door of the blue bedroom when she heard a sound that spiked a chill between her shoulders.

Across the landing, within the red bedroom, came the angry shaking of a cage's metal bars.

Then a female voice, muffled by the closed door, said soothingly, 'Shall I slice some cheek for you next, my sable princeling? Or would you prefer a cut of neck? There, you do enjoy it juicy and dripping, don't you? Dearest pusskin, darling Catesby.'

Grace took a nervous step sideways and in doing so nudged the table. It banged against the wall and the voice fell silent. The girl bit her lip. Presently the door of the red bedroom opened slightly and a middle-aged woman's sharp face appeared, with a pinched nose and dark, suspicious eyes.

'Mrs Axmill,' Grace said. 'I was just taking the master's ward his supper.'

The housekeeper withdrew her face in order to glance over her shoulder. The gas lamps in that room were turned down and Grace couldn't make out anything except the domed silhouette of the cage. Without opening the door any wider, Mrs Axmill manoeuvred herself on to the landing, deftly sweeping the bustle of her prim black dress behind her. When she had turned the key in the lock, she directed her wintry stare at Grace once more.

'That will be all, Flossy,' she instructed. '*I* will take the tray in to Master Verne.'

'It's no trouble, Mrs Axmill.'

'Has the summer heat made you deaf, girl?'

'No, Mrs Axmill. There's a baked apple dumpling to come as well.'

The pinched nose sniffed with distaste. 'He won't care for that,' the housekeeper said flatly. 'Don't bother bringing it up.'

'You sure? He must eat something, he's wasting away, poor lamb. Could a doctor not be called?'

Mrs Axmill glared at her, stung by her impertinence.

'Don't speak out of turn, girl! It's not your place to comment on the health and well-being of your employers. Return below and be about your duties. If you don't have enough work to occupy your time, I can easily furnish you with more.'

Grace lowered her eyes to hide the insolent gleam which she knew would be burning in them. Her glance fell upon the starched white cuff jutting from the housekeeper's sleeve. There was a vivid smear of blood across it.

'You've cut yourself bad!' she exclaimed.

The housekeeper looked down at her cuff in consternation and covered the bright scarlet streak with her hand.

'Don't be foolish,' she rebuked her. 'It's from the meat I was feeding the marquess's pet.'

'Oh,' Grace said, staring anxiously back at the red room's closed door. 'Can I ask, Mrs Axmill, what sort of creature is in there? I've heard how some lordly gentlemen keep savage beasts, like tigers and lions. In olden days they say the famous Captain Scoresby brought a polar bear back to Whitby aboard one of his whaling ships, and it escaped and rampaged through the town. It's not a bear or lion in there, is it? I'm just fearful if the cage don't prove all it should be and it gets loose . . .'

'A bear? A lion? Can you hear how absurd you are, girl? I credited you with owning more wits than that. Nevertheless, the master's pet darling is no concern of yours. Now, do as I've bid you.'

Grace hurried down the stairs obediently. She was glad to get away from the vicinity of that door, but her lively mind was troubled and those worries increased as the evening wore on.

Much later she lay in bed, too uncomfortable to sleep. The August weather had made the attics stifling, but remembering what Esme had said, she was afraid to open the skylight. And yet it wasn't just the airless fug beneath the rafters that kept her awake.

She could not believe the young master would turn his nose up at an apple dumpling. What boy would? Either of her two little brothers, or any of the other tykes she had grown up with over on the East Cliff, would wolf it down in two great bites. For some time, Grace had harboured the unpleasant suspicion that Mrs Axmill was starving the child, and now Mrs Paddock was beginning to believe it too. Grace doubted if he had even seen the curried mutton. But why would the housekeeper do such a thing? And if he was genuinely sick, why refuse to call the doctor? Strong-willed and gentle-hearted, Grace refused to stand back and allow this to continue. She had resolved to do something about the situation, beginning this very night.

The other worry that kept sleep at bay concerned the meat Mrs Axmill had been feeding the unseen beast. The brightness of the blood told how fresh it was, but Grace was certain that, apart from the mutton shoulder which went into the curry, not so much as a cutlet had passed through the kitchen all that day or yesterday. So where had it come from?

It was just before midnight when she heard the coach bringing the marquess back to the hall. She felt sorry for Jed, the groom. He wouldn't get any rest until the horses had been dealt with and the carriage washed of mud and the woodwork polished. Mrs Paddock had left some cold cuts in the kitchen if they hadn't fed him in the servants' hall of Mulgrave Castle, but knowing Jed, he'd eat them even if they had.

Grace crept to her door and opened it slightly. Sounds carried easily up the great central stairwell of Bagdale Hall. She heard heavy boots striding through the entrance far below and two voices. One was Mrs Axmill; she had waited up for the marquess's return. Grace pulled a face. The way the housekeeper fawned over the new master was nauseating. The other voice belonged to the marquess himself. In spite of the heat, Grace shivered. In private his manner was arrogant and ugly, yet she had heard how it changed in the presence of visitors. 'Like wedding cake dipped in honey,' Mrs Paddock had described it, and she was right.

Standing in her nightdress, her hair hanging loose past her shoulders, the girl continued to listen. The boots stomped up the stairs to the landing below. There was a barked command, dismissing Mrs Axmill, then Grace heard the red bedroom being

21

unlocked. The noises grew indistinct and she knew he had gone in to see his savage pet. Some minutes later the sounds were clearer as he emerged once more, but who was he speaking to now?

The girl opened her door a little wider and put her head out. The cramped attic landing was pitch-dark, but a bobbing radiance below made the banisters stand out stark and black. Grace guessed the marquess was carrying an oil lamp.

'One night soon,' he snapped, 'the parcel will be delivered to the appointed place. Your wits, such as they are, need to be clear. No helping yourself to the port and brandy, you understand? Since you've been under this roof, you've done little else but drink yourself into stupors.'

Grace couldn't hear any response, but the new master continued as if there had been one.

'See that it finds its way into the right hands. It must be given to the town hag in good faith – she must suspect nothing. I can't so much as touch it. Do you think I'd entrust this task to a rancid sot like you if I could?'

There was a pause. Whoever he was talking to spoke in such a low whisper it was impossible to hear.

'You'd better be, else I'll cut off those great ears of yours and choke you with them. Now sleep it off – you reek like the floor of an alehouse privy.'

Grace heard the door of his own bedchamber open

and close and the light was quenched. On the landing there was a crash as the side table was kicked over in a temper.

'Who's down there?' she murmured, closing her own door again and returning to bed where she hugged her knees and waited.

The night deepened and Bagdale Old Hall eventually sank into complete silence.

When she thought enough time had elapsed, Grace fumbled in the dark along her bedside shelf. She had taken some thick slices of ham, a wedge of pork pie and an apple from the kitchen and wrapped them in a handkerchief. Her plan was to creep downstairs and place them beside the young master's bed. If Mrs Axmill was withholding his meals, she wouldn't be able to stop him enjoying this little feast when he discovered it.

Clasping the bundle in one hand, she eased her door open and, in her bare feet, stepped silently past Mrs Paddock's room, which resonated with the chuffing of the cook's steam-engine-like snores.

At the top of the stairs Grace hesitated. If she was caught doing this she would lose her position, but she would almost welcome that. However, having to face the new master's temper was a different matter; that really was something to be afraid of. Long moments passed as she pushed aside the dread of that encounter. It was the thought of young Verne going hungry which spurred her on.

Hardly daring to breathe, she descended, taking extra care as she passed the master's room. No sound at all came from there, not even the gentlest of snores. That unnerved Grace more than ever. He must sleep like the dead, or perhaps he was still awake, although no light was showing under the door.

The first-floor landing was black as the grave. She had been here countless times during the day, but in this blind darkness it was alarmingly unfamiliar and she groped for the wall to guide her. The still, warm air smelled faintly of brandy and she recalled the one-sided conversation she had overheard. Where was that unknown person the marquess had been speaking to? Before her thoughts could dwell on that, she struck her shin so hard she dropped the food bundle and let out a sharp yelp.

Her voice shattered the profound silence and she cursed the object she had blundered into. Crouching, she reached out and discovered it was the overturned side table. Hardly daring to breathe, she waited to see if her clumsiness had attracted attention. Those anxious moments seemed endless, but there was no other sound in the house.

Grace bowed her head as relief flooded through her knotted muscles and she rubbed her painful shin. Then she frantically searched the darkness, hunting for the dropped bundle. Fortunately it hadn't rolled far. Snatching it up, she navigated around the table and cautiously edged towards the blue bedroom.

Locating the door, she delicately patted her hand over it to find the brass handle. Then she froze. Behind her, the lock of the red bedroom clicked. A waft of cool air blew on to her neck and a flickering stripe of dim yellow light appeared on the wall beside her.

Her heart thudding, she turned slowly. The door of the forbidden room, where that mystery creature was kept hidden, was now ajar and, as she stared in mounting dread, it opened wider – seemingly by itself.

'Mrs Axmill?' she ventured fearfully. 'Is that you? I was . . . I thought . . .'

But she couldn't think of an excuse to justify her presence here at this ungodly hour.

The expected scornful censure never came, just more silence. Unnerved, Grace peered into the room. She couldn't see anyone within. On the large table, beside the cage, an oil lamp was burning. Mustering all her courage, she put the food bundle down and stepped forward.

'Mrs Axmill?' she repeated. 'You in there? Or . . . or is it you, my lord?'

Still no answer.

Grace's curiosity began to master her fear. Reaching the doorway, she hesitated on the threshold, frowning at the shadow-filled corners. Were they dark enough to conceal someone? Her sharp eyes detected no lurking figure, but they drank in other details.

The rugs had been rolled up and empty bottles littered the room. It looked as if the unknown drinker had guzzled half the wine cellar. Most of them were crowded round an untidy heap of blankets that someone had been using as a bed, the real one having been dismantled and stacked against the wall. But marks of savagery were everywhere. Were they the result of drunken rages? No, it was more than that. Propped against the panelling, the mattress had been slashed to tatters, the horsehair stuffing spilled out in tangled clumps and the floorboards were gouged with deep scratches. To Grace's astonishment the vicious scoring continued up the walls. In several places the wainscoting was nothing but splinters. With a shock she saw that even the ceiling had not escaped the frenzied attacks, and laths were jutting through the clawed plaster. But how did any creature get up there?

The girl turned her attention to the only other feature in that ruined space. Made from ornate ironwork, in the shape of a classical Greek temple with gilded details, was the largest cage she had ever seen. It was easily big enough to hold a lion. Standing on the central table it reared above her, the dome almost reaching the ravaged ceiling.

A fringed cloth was draped over the near side, concealing the beast within. Grace's imagination raced. What was in there? She couldn't hear any breathing.

Edging closer, she squeezed her hands together to stop them shaking and warily drew back the cloth. The cage was empty.

The shock made her jump. Picking up the oil lamp, she saw that the metal gate was open and for one horrible moment thought the animal was loose in the room with her. Then she realised where the draught was coming from.

'It climbed out the window,' she whispered. 'Or . . . or flew out.'

Grace shrank back. She had to get away from Bagdale Hall. There was an overwhelming presence of evil here. But who would believe her?

'Nannie Burdon,' she whispered. 'She will. She'll know what to do. I'll go see her.'

Replacing the lamp on the table, she noticed for the first time an object that resembled a large hat. Bringing the light closer she realised it was a plate, and a dark cloth covered the bulky object on it. A sharp knife nearby and the smell of blood told Grace that this was the meat Mrs Axmill had been feeding to the creature earlier. Unable to stop herself, she reached for the edge of the cloth and raised it. The lamplight shone over what lay beneath.

A strangled shriek scratched out of the girl's throat. 'Esme!'

Reeling from the grisly horror she had unveiled, Grace stumbled out of the room and on to the landing, where she saw that the side table was now upright. The handkerchief bundle was on top of it, untied, and a large bite had been taken from the pork pie. An uncorked bottle of brandy slid across the table on its own and a filthy laugh mocked her from thin air.

Grace screamed and fled down the dark stairs.

Flinging herself across the hall she wrenched at the front door, but it was secured by three large iron bolts.

'Save and protect me!' she prayed aloud, reaching up to drag the topmost across. 'Please Lord, help me! Send an angel to protect me from the devils and demons of this house!'

Stooping to pull the lowest bolt clear, she heard slippered footsteps hurrying along the passage from the housekeeper's room.

Wrapped in an expensive silk dressing gown that had belonged to her former mistress, Mrs Axmill burst into in the hallway. With steel-grey hair plaited in a heavy cable down her back, her face was slathered in so much cold cream that she looked like a greasy apparition.

'Have you taken leave of your senses, girl?' she bawled. 'Return to your room at once! How dare you shriek down the household at this hour of the night.'

'Stay away from me!' Grace shouted back, struggling with the middle bolt. 'Murderers is what you are! Monsters! You and the master! I saw – I saw what you did to poor Esme!'

Mrs Axmill's fierce expression vanished immediately and was replaced by a stony derision, which was even more alarming.

'You should not have gone into that room,' she said with icy finality. 'Why can't you silly girls ever do as you're told? So foolish.'

Grace wiped her frightened tears away.

'I'll fetch the law on you!'

A sinister smile appeared in the cold cream.

'You won't be telling anyone anything, Flossy,' Mrs Axmill threatened.

'My name is Grace!'

'No,' the housekeeper corrected her with a vicious grin. '"Dead" is what you are.'

Snarling, she leaped at her, seizing the girl by the throat.

Grace tried to fight back, but the housekeeper was stronger than she looked and the girl crumpled beneath her.

'Who would believe a snot-nosed slum slattern like you anyway?' Mrs Axmill growled through bared teeth as she squeezed her fingers tighter round the slender neck.

Gasping for breath, Grace kicked and pushed, but it was futile. In choking desperation she grabbed the woman's long plait and tore at it.

Mrs Axmill screeched and Grace punched her in the stomach. The grip loosened from the girl's throat and she shoved her away. Mrs Axmill spun into the wall, splatting cold cream where her face smacked the panels. Incensed, she came raging back, launching at Grace like a tigress.

But Grace was ready. She had snatched a silver-topped walking cane from the cloak stand and swung it defiantly. It cracked Mrs Axmill across the skull and she howled as she crashed to the floor.

Grace drew the final bolt free, yanked the door open and raced into the night.

Clutching her head, Mrs Axmill lurched to her feet and headed for the stairs.

'My lord!' she called urgently. 'My lord!'

Reaching the marquess's bedchamber, she was about to pound on his door when it opened and the master of the house stood glowering at her.

The Marquess Darqueller was a tall, athletic man. She worshipped his strong, handsome face, with its penetrating velvet black eyes that seemed to see into those deepest, most secret places she had kept hidden from the world for so long. He was half dressed, his shirt was undone and his thick raven hair pleasingly untidy.

Even through the hammering pain between her

temples, Mrs Axmill took a moment to admire him. She was so completely in his power.

'What is it?' he demanded.

'The maid, Flossy. She's been in the red room.'

'And you let her get away?'

'She attacked me and struck me down. I'm sorry, my lord.'

Her master pushed by and ran across the landing.

'Rouse the boy!' he ordered the housekeeper. 'Don't bother to dress him – there is no time.'

Mrs Axmill hurried to obey, but glanced back before entering Master Verne's room. The marquess was speaking angrily to what appeared to be an empty corner, where an empty bottle of brandy lay on the floor.

'I warned you, Gull!' he growled, his fists trembling with barely contained fury. 'I said leave the drink alone. You're stewed! Don't strain my patience further! The humans in this hall are not here for your amusement, you stunted, mollusc-brained halfwit. I don't care how curious she was – I would have dealt with it. I had a particular use in mind for that girl; she was not for you to play with!'

Frowning at those last words, Mrs Axmill rubbed her aching head and entered the blue bedroom.

'Get up, Master Verne,' she shouted, clapping her hands. 'Wake up!'

Another thick, low fog, what the locals called a 'fret', had rolled in off the sea. It flooded the labyrinth lanes of Whitby with dense grey vapour. In some places it was waist-deep; in others it crept up the walls and pressed against bedroom windows.

Fleeing Bagdale Hall, casting the walking cane aside, Grace rushed up Spring Hill, scything a path through the curdling mist. The police station wasn't far. If there was no one on duty at this hour she would batter on the door until she woke the inspector in his house or one of the unmarried constables in the rooms above.

Cocooned in fog, the red-brick building was just in view when a tall, burly figure in a caped coat strode into sight ahead. The gaslight of a street lamp behind him pitched his bearded face into shadow, but the girl could tell from his homburg hat that he wasn't a policeman.

'You there!' he challenged her, in a gruff Irish brogue. 'What are you doing out at this hour?'

Grace's mind was in turmoil, whirling with the horror she had witnessed in the red bedroom. Halting, she stared at the stranger fearfully and was about to cry for help when he raised his arm and she saw a revolver in his hand.

A shot exploded from the muzzle. It thundered

high over her head. Grace spun round and tore back down the hill. Only one thought blazed brightly now: she had to get home, across the river, to her father's cottage on the East Cliff.

'Stop!' the man yelled behind her. 'Wait there! Stop!'

Grace didn't even hear him. Panic and terror drove her. She ran like a hare through Baxtergate. No glimmer of light shone in the windows of the surrounding buildings and the blanketing fog obscured the road. Stones cut her bare feet and she almost twisted her ankle when she crashed against the unseen kerb.

The quay was just ahead. One dash through Old Market Place, then over the bridge, and home and safety would be moments away. Yet she knew she would never be free of the hideous sight she had uncovered in that forbidden room. That ghastly horror would haunt her forever and thinking of it now made her feel sick.

'What's this, what's this?' a hearty voice greeted her. 'Why have you strayed from the snuggery of your bed, little miss?'

Another man had emerged from the shadowy mist into her path. Grace tried to dodge aside, but he hooked her arm and reeled her back towards him.

'What's sent you dashing through these dark streets as though your chemise were on fire?' he asked.

The girl struggled.

'Hold easy, lass!' he chuckled. 'Rufus Brodribb won't harm you none. He saves his pugilism for the dough in the bakery. What's got you so frighted? You're quailing like a cornered mouse in the grain store.'

Gulping desperate breaths, Grace looked up at him. She saw a thin but benign and ruddy face, flanked by a profusion of ginger side whiskers and a pair of pince-nez on a long nose. His shirt sleeves were rolled past the elbow and over his waistcoat he wore a large white apron.

'Honest Rufus Brodribb, presently of Botham's baker's,' he introduced himself with a friendly grin. 'But most others do call me Crusty Rustychops, on account of me trade and the luxuriance of me cheek ticklers. What say you and me cut along to the place  of my employment, where you can regale my ears with your troubles over a pot of tea and a fresh-made pastry? As me old mam used to say, "Nowt looks so bad over the brim of a china cup." 'Tis not far.'

Grace squirmed in his grasp. 'I must get on home!' she protested. 'It's not safe out here. Let go, he'll be after me!'

'Who, lass?'

'The master!' she cried. 'They're killers, her an' him! They murdered Esme – butchered her! And there's another out here, back that way – with a gun. Mercy save me! They cut her head clean off!'

The baker stared at her in disbelief.

'What are you saying?' he asked, and the bantering tone was gone from his voice. 'Tell me. Be quick!'

Before she could answer, a shrill mewling sounded in the sky.

'God's teeth!' he declared, scanning the heavens as a black shape flew across the stars. 'What in thunderation was that?'

'It's what were in the cage,' Grace muttered.

'Cage? Where is this cage? Tell me, child!'

Grace shook her head in confusion. The baker was no longer speaking in a Yorkshire accent.

Two shots rang out. The noise ricocheted through the cramped lanes, seeming to come from every direction.

Rufus Brodribb whirled about and gave a snort of annoyance.

'What is the blessed fool doing?' he snapped. 'I told him no wild shooting tonight!'

Grace grabbed her chance. She pulled herself free and raced into the mist, towards the quayside. Brodribb was about to give chase when another shot blasted into the night, followed by a man's bellowing yell. This time there was no doubt: it came from somewhere near Bagdale.

'By God's eyelid!' he declared impatiently.

It was too late to pursue the frightened girl. The billowing vapour had swallowed her. He would never find her in that. Taking a small pistol from his waistcoat pocket he hurried back along Baxtergate.

Grace was lost in a fog bank. This close to the river it was thicker than ever and she could barely see her hands in front of her face. Finding a wall, she warily edged her way alongside it until she reached a corner. There was nothing she could do but follow it round. Soon she encountered a row of barrels and heard the clank and rattle of rigging close by. Grace realised she was perilously near the quayside and would have to take care not to step off the edge and plunge into the water.

Cautiously, she continued on her way. The Scottish herring fleet had departed early this year and more barrels than usual crowded the quay. It was slow work, picking her way along, but a breath of wind moved over the waters and the mist began to thin until Grace could get her bearings. She was dismayed to discover she was only behind Collier's, the chandler's and ironmonger's, and that the bridge was still a little distance away. Hurrying forward she was astonished to see a small, familiar figure standing upon one of the barrels ahead.

It was a boy in his nightshirt; in his hands he held a beautiful round object made from shining gold.

'Master Verne!' exclaimed Grace. 'Thanks be! How did you escape? What are you doing here and what have you there? Don't say you stole it from the master!'

There was no recognition in his wide, staring eyes and no answer came from his lips.

'It's Grace,' she told him. 'You know me. Come, take my hand. We'll both get out of this nasty fret and put my dad's stout door 'tween us and the horrors of Bagdale Hall. Get you fed as well. You're fair starved, poor lad.'

Still no reply, but the boy's dark pupils drifted from her anxious face to a tall shape that jumped down from the barrels behind her.

'He knows you best as Flossy surely?' came the unmistakable snarl of the marquess. 'Do not confuse my ward any more than he already is. His young mind is as befogged as these streets. Mrs Axmill is a most efficient housekeeper and has many superior qualities for a female of her time and station, but she founders in the management of young boys. The laudanum bottle is a poor substitute for a governess. However, it and a spartan diet keep him subdued and biddable. He used to be so defiant and mutinous.'

Grace turned slowly.

Cloaked with curling mist, the Marquess

Darqueller towered before her. An ugly sneer twisted his handsome face and cruelty beyond measure beat from those pitiless eyes.

Grace felt faint. She sensed his domineering will strike at her spirit, trying to subjugate and crush her personality, to control her thoughts. But she refused to be cowed and turned her fear to anger.

'Don't you come near me!' she shouted. 'I'll scream this town out of their beds, telling everyone what you done – and scratch such a mark on you you'll never be rid of it.'

'Don't show your claws to me, kitten,' he said with a foul laugh. 'I have sharper barbs.'

Reaching into the pocket of his tailcoat he brought out a lozenge-shaped leather case, from which he took a syringe.

'Blood is the bridge,' he told her. 'I had planned to wait a few weeks more before this intimate moment, but your incurable inquisitiveness, coupled with the inebriate tendencies of my unseen house guest, have advanced matters.'

Grace shrank back.

'You're mad!' she cried. 'But they'll hang you anyways – you and Axmill. You'll both twitch at the end of ropes. Keep that needle away from me.'

'I do not fear the gallows. I have already danced that jig.'

Grace threw back her head to scream, but terror

killed her voice. Leathery wings swooped down out of the fog. Razor claws dug into her scalp and a ferocious feline face spat into her eyes.

Grace whirled around wildly, trying to drag the creature from her head.

'Play dainty, Catesby,' the marquess said. 'Don't spoil its beauty. I want the corpse to be a comely one, not riven with scars and stitches like your own patched and lumpen carcass.'

Striding up to the girl, he raised his hand.

A tear carved a path down Verne's cheek as he watched Grace lose her frantic battle and fall to the ground.

Smirking, the marquess knelt beside her and brushed the auburn tresses away from her throat. Blue sparks crackled between his thumb and forefinger as he rubbed them together and by their bouncing light he admired the exposed neck.

'Such a pretty one,' he observed as he set about filling the syringe with blood.

Moments later he held the scarlet fluid aloft. 'Behold, Catesby. The first of our dowries, the bonniest of bride prices.'

Before he could say more, the mist echoed with urgent, running footsteps.

'You certain you saw it fly this way?' a panting voice asked.

'I'd swear to that,' came the insistent reply.

Returning the syringe to its case, the marquess gazed down at Grace's body. For the present he had what he needed. Stepping over to Verne, he snapped his fingers at Catesby.

'Divert them,' he instructed.

The large sable creature spread its wide bat wings and pounced into the air. Soaring up, it skimmed the ironmonger's chimney and zigzagged over the road beyond, screeching its unearthly cry.

'There!' one of the voices called.

A gunshot split the night.

'You'll never hit it,' the other man declared. 'And even if you did, would a mere bullet have any effect? God's teeth, what misshapen devils plague this little town? What malignant canker has taken root?'

Hearing them, the marquess laughed softly to himself. Standing behind Verne, he gripped the boy's shoulders.

Verne lifted the golden Nimius and they rose off the quayside, flying silently into the fog that hung low over the harbour.

Keeping Catesby in view, the two armed men turned into Flowergate.

'It's over the fields behind the Union Mill is where that hellspawn will be heading,' said the burly, bearded Irishman. 'Where it eluded me the last time.'

'Hellspawn?' repeated his companion with the

ginger side whiskers. 'What has become of the rationalist and his steadfast belief in a natural, scientific explanation for the events here?'

'When a fiend fresh out of Hades knocks your hat off, only a dunce would claim it was the wind. No one's ever seen anything like that before.'

'Mark the way it wheels about up there. Why such brazen dilly-dallying? I find that singularly suspicious.'

'You think we're being led by the nose? To what intent?'

'I believe we should heed the counsel of Friar Lawrence in the Romeo tragedy: *Wisely and slow. They stumble that run fast.*'

The Irishman scratched his beard. 'Was that not a caution against falling in love?'

'It is a prudent maxim for every hazardous circumstance.'

'And if, against all scientific reason, we should find that bullets do indeed prove useless against that agent of evil? What do we do then?'

Brodribb raised his thick brows dramatically and peered over his pince-nez at him.

'Why then, my friend,' he said with zeal, 'we do our Christian and theatrical best.'

Staring back down Flowergate towards the harbour, a spasm of concern clouded his face.

'I pray that young girl reached home safely. If only she had disclosed more. The blame is entirely mine; I should not have dropped out of character. These are the murkiest and deepest waters we have ever waded in. But come – let us hunt our quarry through field and thicket and, as I always say when we embark upon these perilous undertakings, *Here's to our enterprise*!'

On the quayside, Grace Pickering's discarded body lay by the barrels. Her blood trickled in a vivid stream over the flagstones until it reached the edge, where it dripped into the river.

2

Stone scraping against stone, vigorous, from side to side, side to side. Early morning sunlight filtering through lightly closed lashes. A mind rising slowly from darkness.

'*Voolyvoo, mamzel,*' said a cheery voice. '*Hola, senior rita.*'

Lil stirred. Her head was swimming and she groaned at the dull aches that clamped every joint of her body.

'How about a kiss?'

She opened her eyes. The world was a blurred jumble of light, with a garish splodge of colour in the centre.

'Show us your bloomers,' the colours said, followed by a wolf whistle.

Lil blinked and wiped the sleep away. The bleary vision gradually came into focus and she found herself in a small living room, lying on a wide settle covered in patchwork cushions. Ogling her, from the back of a wooden armchair, was a large parrot with vibrant red, blue and yellow plumage.

'Wh . . . where am I?' Lil murmured, her voice cracked and parched.

'Doris!' it squawked, fanning its beautiful wings and bobbing its head up and down. 'Doris! Where's Doris?'

'What's going on?' Lil rasped. Putting a hand to her head she discovered that her skin was covered in a vile-smelling dark green ointment.

'Doris!'

'Shove a cork in it, George,' a woman's voice called from the ajar front door. 'Else I'll make meself a bobby-dazzler hat out of your feathers and feed what's left to next door's tabby.'

'DORIS!'

'Shut up, you gormless kipper's armpit! Can't you see I'm scouring me step?'

The woman bustled into the room, brandishing a large lump of sandstone. The parrot raised one foot off the chair back and waved it at her.

'Give us a kiss,' he said.

'Come Christmas you'll be stuffed with sage and onion,' she cooed, her soft tone at odds with her harsh words as she tickled him behind the head. 'No more uncoutheries from you to make me choke on me chestnuts.'

Then she noticed Lil was sitting up.

'Finally awake and compost mental then,' she stated, folding her arms and pursing her lips like a terse trout.

Lil tried to answer, but her mouth was too dry.

'I know what you need. The lad with the milk donkey's already been so I've got some in. Wait there.'

She disappeared into the kitchen and returned with a full cup, which Lil accepted gratefully.

'Best cure for the derangement your innards have been through,' the woman said, nodding approvingly. 'Can't stand the stuff meself, seeing as it's just cow squeezings. I can just about tolerate a spot in a cup of tea – and stout of course.'

'What happened?' Lil asked when she had drained it. 'I don't know where I am. How did I get here?'

'Still a bit bepuddled, are you? You're in my front room, lady, that's where you are – wearing my second-best nightie I'll have you know. There's some porridge in the pot. I dare say your giblets will be rumbling.'

'Who are you?'

'Folk round here call me Nannie Burdon, them as don't disgarage me worse behind my back, that is. Proper name is Nellie. It's only George what calls me Doris, I don't know why, but he's a cheeky birdbrain with no manners and a suppository of lewd language that makes the vicar blench. He used to belong to a ship's captain – George, not the vicar. Happen Doris must've been the captain's particular lady friend at one time and the name stuck and there's no winkling it out of him. Any road up, this cockadoodle of many colours and a monkey in a sailor suit were all the old salty gentleman had left when he were ferried away on his final celestial voyage. I took the bird on as no one else were daft enough to have him. That were nigh on twenty year ago and the foul-mouthed fowl still hasn't devulgarised his repertoire – makes me want to scrub his beak out with carbolic. I should have chose the monkey. I might've trained that hairy fella to dust the webs off the ceiling or do a party piece at Christmas, maybe a jaunty little dance with a paper hat on, or juggle a few nuts, summat of that nature. Instead, what do I get every year? A scandalacious limerick about a tattooed dancer in Nantucket. Puts you clean off your pudding and Boxing Day can't come round fast enough.'

She paused to draw breath and looked Lil up and down appraisingly. George uttered a cackling, 'Hur hur.'

'So,' the woman resumed. 'With whom am I currently having the pleasure?'

Lil viewed her with just as much curiosity. Nannie Burdon was a short and dumpy woman, shaped like a Russian nesting doll, possibly in her late sixties, with tightly curled dark hair streaked with grey. Her face showed a hard-lived life, yet it was so mobile and expressive it presented a comic quality and her eyes gleamed like steel buttons, always darting around, keenly alive with interest. A navy blue woollen shawl was wrapped around her narrow shoulders and crossed over her bosom. Her voluminous brown skirt reached past her ankles and the scuffed toes of old boots were just visible beneath the hem. The area about her knees displayed two large dusty patches, attesting to the daily chore of keeping the front step immaculate, which was of paramount importance to the dwellers of these cottages.

'I've heard of you,' Lil said, trying to remember where.

'Have you now? Well, we'll come to that later. At the risk of regurgitating myself, what's your name?'

'Sorry, I'm, er . . . Lil, I think . . . Yes, Lil Wilson.'

'Oh, is it now? Well, I've told folk round here you're a Burdon from Middlesbrough, so that's what you'll be for as long as you're under my roof. So where are you really from, Lilian?'

'It's not Lilian. It's Lilith, but just call me Lil. I'm from a town called Whitby. Where is this? Can I have my clothes?'

'No you can't.'

'Why?'

'Because I burned them. Ooh, I couldn't risk having them about the place. They might be discriminating.'

'You burned my clothes?'

'They weren't fit for human habitation and them funny shoes were half melted.'

'My trainers?'

'Ugly, clumpy things, bad as clogs. Were they them special shoes, you know, awfulpedics? Have you got a limp or summat?'

'No, everyone wears them. Look, I know I'm in your front room, but where is that exactly?'

'Hold your hosses! Let me sit down and take the weight off my various veins. I saved the continents of your pockets – they're down here. I made certain sure they weren't perturbed.'

Nannie Burdon sat in the chair and George hopped on to her shoulder as she reached for a sewing basket by the fireplace. Lil regarded her with growing impatience. The muddled vocabulary was irritating and she seemed incapable of remaining still for a moment. It was as if some internal, imperfectly balanced motor would not switch off. She twitched and fidgeted, fiddled with a blouse button or patted a curl or squirmed in her seat or pulled her mouth into strange shapes.

'Here's an odd little clasp or brooch,' the woman said, holding up Lil's polymer clay witch badge. 'Why's it got a green face? Is it sickening for summat? Is that a turnip lantern it's holding? Where'd you get such an article? Not what you'd call handsome.

Wouldn't catch me wearing owt like that, nor anyone else round here.'

'I made it.'

Nannie Burdon sniffed sceptically. 'Make a lot of jewellery no one would want to wear, does you? Seems an infertile pastime to me.'

'I make plenty – and we sell lots in my family's shop. Although . . . I haven't actually made that one yet.'

'You must've walloped your head very hard. So what's this then? Is it a carry case for holding them diddy calling cards? "Lord Ponsonby Smythe did pop round while you was out having your toffee nose sharpened and your pantaloons polished, your ladymuckness." I couldn't open it.'

'It's my phone! Hope you haven't broken it.'

'Your what?'

'My phone.'

'What's one of them when it's at home?'

The question took Lil by surprise. She gazed around the room. It was sparsely furnished: no carpet, just bare stone flags, with a rag rug in front of the hearth. On the mantle between two brass candlesticks was a small clock, and above that a little circular mirror. There were no pictures or photographs on the yellowing walls, but two shelves in the chimney alcove displayed an odd assortment of crockery. Matchboarding ran round the lower half of the walls, waxed and polished a rich shade of ginger. With a shock, Lil realised there was no electric light overhead, merely an oil lamp hanging from a hook.

'Then there's this,' Nannie Burdon continued, scrutinising the girl's expression as she lifted out a string of three ammonites.

'My necklace!'

'Is that all it is to you, a neck knick-knack? Nothing more?'

'Why ask that?'

The woman raised her eyebrows and gave a knowing chuckle. She reached into the collar of her blouse and pulled out a similar necklace, except that the ammonites on hers were made from jet.

'Because I've got one as well,' she declared.

'Now I know who you are!' Lil cried. 'I've seen your name on a list – a list of . . .' she lowered her voice '. . . witches.'

She stared about the room once more, then out of the window at the courtyard beyond. Much of it was different yet at the same time very familiar.

'This cottage!' she exclaimed. 'I've been in it before, a long time from now. There should be lava lamps on that mantelpiece and a glass coffee table over there, with a Trimphone on it, and a stereogram along that wall, playing T. Rex.'

'Are you having an aberration?' Nannie Burdon asked, with a baffled look. 'What were in that milk? I might have a sup of that meself after all.'

'I'm saying this is a witch's cottage and that necklace belongs to me for the same reason yours does to you.'

'Oh, think you're a titchy witch, do you? Where'd you get it?'

'I *know* I'm a witch, a knot witch, and the previous owner gave me that, her sign of office. She was from way further back than whenever this is and I carry a part of her in me still.'

'Sounds like indigestion; sooner you get some porridge down you the better.'

Lil scowled at her. 'What kind of witch are you?'

Nannie Burdon looked about the room as if someone else might be listening and shifted awkwardly on the chair. George leaned in closer.

'I'm a bottle witch,' she murmured.

'What's one of them?'

'It's nothing swanky or flame-boying. I just have a knack for concoctivating plants and suchlike. I brew and I pickle, make healing ointments, philtres and lotions. When folk can't afford the doctor they come here, and I does them more good than one of them ever could. Bottling is one of the oldest forms of the craft there is, same as yours. Though I wish you was in the time guild – only them should go paddling in yesterdays and tomorrows. No saying what apostrophes you can cause here.'

'I don't want to make any trouble,' Lil promised.

'What are you doing here then?'

The girl thumped her thigh in annoyance. 'I've no idea! I know there's something I've got to do, something very important. I just . . . I just can't remember what it is . . .'

'The privies are outside. Use the one on the left. The Swales tykes are always in and out of t'others and like as not there's jam or treacle on the seats. The little mad allicks. Oh, and since the bolt fell off, you have to keep your foot rammed against the door as well, as singing don't deter as it should.'

'I didn't mean that. I just wish I knew why I came here. Can you help me? I don't belong in this time.'

'You want me to help you? I'd say that was dependulent on what you want and who sent you. Were it *Them*? Is it some sort of castigation? Have you been tribunalled?'

'I'm sure no one *sent* me,' Lil began, closing her eyes and trying to break through the haze clouding her memory. 'It was night-time . . . there was a huge bonfire, blazing bright blue . . . a box of watercolours . . . giant red beetles . . . yellow plague . . . a mechanical man – Jack – Jack Potts . . .'

Her voice petered out as the events on the pier that harrowing night in her own time came crashing back in a devastating wave and she remembered everything. 'Cherry!' she yelled in a voice so wrung with anguish that the parrot retreated to the chair back again and fluffed out his feathers. 'Mister Dark killed her! And Verne – he took Verne! I tried to follow them, to get him back. I went on that path of flames . . .'

Covering her face, she sobbed into her hands as the pent-up grief was finally unleashed.

Nannie Burdon let her weep. It was obvious the child had been through a horrendous ordeal so she waited patiently. Her young guest had said enough to set her own thoughts poking into forgotten corners. When she was a girl herself, one of the threats that kept naughty children in check was the promise of a visit from 'Mister Dark'. She hadn't recalled that bogeyman for many years and she sucked and chewed it over as if it was a nasty-tasting lozenge.

When she felt Lil had sobbed enough she resumed the conversation.

'So you chased a time witch on to one of their cut-throughs as it were snuffing out behind them?' she uttered, shaking her head in disbelief. 'I'm just a simple bottler, I'm not well endowed with showy talents like some and was never learned my letters, but even I know that were a barmy idea. No wonder you was covered in them shiny blebs. You was lucky, lady. You rode time's lashing tail and lived to tell of it. Good thing a little friend of mine guessed summat of the sort and I had an old jar of the right salve doing nothing at the back of a cupboard. Worked a treat by the looks of it. History burns, Lil, forward or back or sideways. But them sores have gone down nicely. You'd have been done for if they hadn't been tended to right away.'

Lil was taking deep breaths, trying to contain the clawing heartbreak and push it deep down to deal with later. There would be a better time for this, but now she had to concentrate on why she was here. She stared at the ointment plastered on her hands and up her arms. It was also on her legs and face.

'This stuff stinks,' she said.

'It didn't when it went on. That's the scum and decomposure it leeched out of you what's doing the reeking. It's the mouldy pong of the years you smashed through. Skipping hither and then don't have no cost, you know. Only the guild can perambulate them ginnels unscathed. You must have come back a long way to be congested with so much decay and smell so bad. What were it, fifty year or so hence?'

'Hang on, I was covered in burns?'

'Like streaky bacon, almost crispy.'

'It just feels a bit like sunburn now. How long have I been out of it?'

'You've been unconspicuous on that there settle for three whole days. I never thought you'd live through the first, you was so bad. Then last night you rounded the bend and the scalds started to fade. Like I said, you was lucky; there must be a strong blessing on you.'

'Three days?' Lil uttered in dismay. 'I'll never catch up with Verne. They could be anywhere now. What's the date?'

'Time for a quick one!' the parrot interjected.

'He don't like to be ignored,' Nannie Burdon explained. 'Has to be the middle of all retention. No one's forgot you, George. We'll be pulling your wishbone after tea tonight, you dandillified duck face.'

'The date?' Lil repeated.

'Twenty-fifth day of August, a Monday, which makes it washday and I've a stack to be doing of, out there in the wash house. Good drying weather though.'

'But the year?'

'It's the year of their lord, eighteen hundred and ninety.'

'So far back,' the girl murmured in wonderment. 'I can't believe it. I'm from . . .'

Nannie Burdon held up a hand.

'Don't go blurting!' she protested. 'Best I don't know. Keep tomorrow's surprises to yourself and don't go telling no one else when you're from neither. I've been putting it about, saying to the sundry how you're a relation what's come to the seaside to get amalgamated and confer less after a dabble of scarlet fever. That should do it and keep the nosy old chatterbags at bay so we can do what's needed.'

'You'll help me then?'

'If I can. It's what we witches are for, protecting this little town. It's what Maudie Dodd did before me and Batty Crow before her and goodness who knows who before that, since time immoral.'

'I have to find out where Mister Dark has gone, where he's taken Verne. Has anyone seen them? Verne is my age, but he looks a bit younger and he's not strong.'

'Tell me more about this Mister Dark.'

'He's a monster!' Lil answered hotly. 'And he isn't a time witch, whatever that is. He's an agent of the Lords of the Deep and has caused so much pain and suffering where I'm from. And now he has the Nimius, the most powerful object in the world. He wouldn't hang around here. He won't be in Whitby.'

'You reckon, do you? Well, let me tell you this, Lady Lil. There's evil sat sitting in this place, been here three months or more and it's getting worse.'

'That can't be him then. He and Verne had only been gone a few moments when I chased after them.'

'Them sparkly ginnels are tricky beggars. A minute at one end could mean a month or a year when you're chucked out t'other. In the meanwhiles, we've had murder, the worst I ever heard of. Two Scottish lasses from the herring fleet was killed, dead as coffin handles, in as many weeks. That's why it sailed off early. Before them there was some poor wretch had his throat ripped out and everything else besides, till not even his own mother would have known him. Not that anybody else would neither; the police and the council have hushed it up between them. Bad for the tripper business over on the West Cliff, you see. No one wants to spend their holidays in them swanky new hotels over there, circumferenced by violent, mysterious deaths, do they?'

She pulled a disgusted face then clasped her hands, almost in prayer, and her bright eyes dimmed.

'And then,' she said, in a soft, wounded voice, 'the night after you appeared, another girl were done in. They found her next morning, not so much as a thimble of blood left. Her name was Grace Pickering, a clever girl, would have done summat with her life, gone places. She grew up here, in this very yard. It were me what delivered her – I was first to hold her, saw her first breath, heard her first cry. So you see, if this Mister Dark of yours is responsible for ending

57

that sweet young life, I'm going to make him pay. I don't care if he is an agent of them Three. I promise, on my witch's oath, I'll have him.'

'I'm sorry about that girl, and the others. I think Mister Dark practises some form of magic based on blood. He killed so many in my time. You wouldn't believe what he did. Wait, he'd have a creature with him, a sort of demonic cat with bat wings, called Catesby.'

'Oh, that's his, is it? Yes, that's been sighted, flying around at night.'

'Then he is here. But I don't get it. Why's he still in Whitby? He's got everything he wants. He doesn't need to stay.'

'There'll be a reason.'

'We find Catesby, we find Dark.'

'But first things first. Grace's death isn't going to be brushed under the rug like them poor herring girls were. They tried to do that at the inquest yesterday. She's having a proper East Cliff send-off. Her fancy-pants employer, him what lives up at Bagdale Hall, offered to put her in his private vault. But no, she'll go in the ground with her dear departed mother. It's only right.'

Rising from the chair, Nannie Burdon pushed her rolled-up sleeves a fraction higher.

'Best get cracking,' she said with determination. 'So much to do today – first there's the Monday wash.

That nightdress will need a lot of elbow work on it so I'll ferret out some clobber for you to change into.'

'Is it safe to wash this green stuff off now?' Lil asked. 'Can I get a shower?'

'I doubt it'll rain today, unless you can make it happen. Can a knot witch do that? Don't you have to whistle or sing or summat?'

Lil smiled. 'That's not what I meant. A bath then?'

'I'll fetch it in for you. It's hanging up outside. There's water heating in the copper, so you're fully abluted. Then you might want to have a traipse round the town and get your bearings. Just be sure you're not back late this afternoon. I've got to get this front room ready for tonight.'

'What's happening tonight?'

'Why, Grace is coming, did I not say?'

'No. You mean the girl who was killed? She's coming here?'

'Course she is. It's the funeral tomorrow and she can't spend the night previous at her dad's. He's useless and wouldn't do it proper. Grace was a child of this yard, so we'll all have a hand in the care of her. Besides, there's the vigil to do.'

'What's that?'

'We're waking her corpse.'

3

To Lil's relief, 'waking a corpse' wasn't what it sounded like. They weren't going to attempt necromancy and bring Grace back from the dead. It was simply a macabre Whitby tradition. Three people, usually female, would sit up all night, keeping watch over the departed, to guard the body from evil forces.

The prospect didn't appeal to her, but Lil understood there would be a lot of strange experiences in store, here in the town's Victorian past. Trying not to think about it, she endured the first of these by washing in a tin bath brought in from outside. It was awkward, uncomfortable and not helped by George perching on one end and squawking every time she reached for the soap. At least afterwards all that green muck had been washed off.

Nannie Burdon rooted out some clothes, which were almost identical to what she herself was wearing, and oversized boots were made to fit with the aid of two thick pairs of heavily darned socks.

When she looked in the small round mirror, Lil was glad the blue streak she once had in her hair had faded: it would have looked very out of place here and would have attracted too much attention. Slipping her necklace on, she picked up her phone and checked it.

'No signal obviously,' she said with a wry smile. 'And only fifteen per cent juice and no way of charging it. Bit useless.'

But she was able to skim through her photos and stared at them sadly. Even if she did manage to find Verne, would they be able to return to their proper time? Would she ever see those faces again? A photo of a laughing Cherry Cerise, in her gaudiest plastic hat and lime-green sunglasses, caused her a stab of sorrow and she flicked past it quickly. A picture of her mother appeared, in full goth gear. Lil turned the phone off and consigned it to her skirt pocket. She wasn't ready to think about Cassandra; she doubted if she'd ever be able to forgive her. Even though her mother had been in Mister Dark's power, too many hurtful things had been said and done, things that could never be taken back or forgotten.

She wrapped a shawl around her shoulders, in spite of the warm day. Nannie Burdon had insisted she put it on. Lil felt nervous about stepping out into the Whitby of 1890 so she fastened her witch badge to the shawl to give herself confidence and make herself feel at home, albeit well over a century adrift in time. If anyone commented on the strangeness of the badge, she had worked out how to explain it away.

With George wolf-whistling at her, she left the cottage.

The yard outside was a forest of hanging washing. There were too many drying lines strung between the dwellings to count, and more laundry was being pegged out as fast as it left the mangle. A gaggle of Whitby wives and widows, gossiping and slandering tradesmen or those in other yards, were gathered by the wash house, arms folded or elbows deep in sloshing tubs. As Lil ducked under the dripping shirts and petticoats, pillowcases and sheets, she felt the burning scrutiny of their curious eyes. Those flushed faced women all wanted to inspect and interrogate her, but Nannie Burdon told them to leave the girl alone: she was 'retrooperating' and had come here for peace and quiet.

Lil was grateful that her hostess wielded a certain authority over her neighbours. Those women looked formidable and she felt sure they would see she was lying about where she was from.

Making her way through the alleyway, she emerged on to Church Street and gazed about her.

It was the weirdest feeling. Just as in Nannie Burdon's home, the place was so familiar and yet very different. This was the same street she had walked down a million times, but it was like seeing it afresh. The bright paintwork and signage of the shops she knew so well were gone, replaced by dark maroon window frames, peeling olive-green doors and drab displays. It looked tired, shabby and sagging, with smoke climbing from almost every chimney, even on a summer day.

There were no goth emporiums or cafes, no concessions made for the interested tourist, just traditional businesses providing the necessities of a bygone age: fruiterers, greengrocers, basket weavers, drapers, staymakers, joiners, bakers, pork butchers, boat builders, coopers, coal merchants, fish curers. This was a solid working town, and every corner was occupied with industry and activity of some sort. The paddle and thrum of treadles and machinery that floated through open windows revealed the location of countless jet works, and the echoing chime of anvils along alleyways announced the presence of blacksmiths.

Market Place was earning its name, with vendors of vegetables, poultry or flowers, and the only people with idle moments were retired fishermen who had been shooed out of doors by busy daughters and sat on stools by their front windows, smoking pipes and watching the world turn, in contemplative acceptance that their involvement was drawing to an end. The reminders of mortality were never far from view: in Church Street alone there were five undertakers. Seeing their windows painted with the words *Funeral requisites at the shortest notice* reminded Lil that death was more commonplace and frequent in the past.

But what astonished her most about this East Cliff was just how much of it would eventually be cleared away. There were far more buildings here, all densely sardined and stacked, with wooden steps leading to galleried upper stories. The bridge end of Church Street was much narrower than she knew it, with more yards, and Grape Lane spilled into a squeezed area called Tin Ghaut, which had been flattened and turned into a car park long before she was born. But there were no cars here and, several times during her exploration, even she lost her bearings.

When she reached Henrietta Street, where she would one day grow up, she found tiered slums jostling for space, in a staggered, terraced descent to the sands. Eventually she stood in front of the cottage that in the future would belong to her family. It seemed small and dingy and she turned away from it to gaze across the harbour.

The first thing she noticed was that the wooden extensions to the stone piers hadn't yet been built and that there were far fewer buildings over on the West

Cliff. Then she did a double take because she couldn't believe what she saw. Rearing high above the roofs of the new hotels was the tower of an immense windmill. Dominating the top of the cliff, it rose from the centre of a long brick building and was higher than the abbey ruins. It was so imposing, the August sunshine appeared to have no power over it. The bricks absorbed the light and remained dark, and the great shadow it cast looked wintry and chill. Curiously it had five sails, but even from this distance they appeared in poor repair.

'Just when you think this place couldn't get any more Gothic, it chucks that impossible thing at you,' Lil spluttered with a giggle. 'It's straight out of a fantasy film – the wizard's fortress and watchtower, high on the rocky crag.'

She looked around to see if anyone was watching. An old woman in a large linen cap was huddled on the grassy bank a short distance away. She was smoking a pipe and gazing out to sea, not even aware of Lil's presence.

Confident no one would notice, the girl removed the phone from her pocket and took some photos of the striking windmill. Then she filmed it and zoomed in.

'Why'd they ever knock it down?' she wondered aloud. 'I've got to get over there and have a proper look. It's amazing.'

'What's amazing?' a voice asked brightly.

Lil turned to see a girl approaching. She was a few years older than Lil; a cotton headscarf was tied tightly under her chin and a hank of mousey hair cascaded down her back. Her eyes were soft green and her cheeks and nose were lightly freckled. She would have been a natural beauty if it wasn't for her teeth. They were large and crooked and she seemed to have difficulty closing her lips over them. A girl from Lil's time might have been self-conscious if a dentist hadn't managed to fix them, but this stranger wasn't afraid to show her friendly smile.

'The windmill,' Lil explained, hastily returning the phone to her pocket. 'I didn't realise Whitby had one.'

'Union Mill? Been shut up and empty since a storm battered it two summers since.'

'That's a shame! It should be repaired and kept standing for a hundred years or so.'

The girl laughed. 'I'd rather they built more grand hotels. I like looking at the well-off ladies and their dresses, with lace like frosty webs and hats that cost more than what my Bill can earn in a year on his dad's boat.'

'Bill your boyfriend?'

There was an enthusiastic nod. 'My intended is what he is. Been courting since we was thirteen, both fifteen now. Just saving to get wed. Maybe in two more years we'll have enough, but I'm not starting married life living with his mother, nor him with mine. That's the road to misery, that is.'

Thinking about those scenarios her smile vanished momentarily, but was soon back.

'Martha Gales,' she introduced herself. 'You'll be Lily Burdon, yes?'

'Lil, but how did you . . .?'

'Nannie Burdon said to keep an eye out for one as looks like she's fresh to this world.'

'She did? And do I really?'

'Oh aye. Middlesbrough's a world and more away

from Whitby, I reckon. I ain't never been. I bet they have lovely frocks in the emporiums there. You ever looked in their windows? I seen pictures in periodicals – oh, but there's some beautiful finery for them what can afford it. I know just what I want on my big day: corded ivory silk with hundreds of tiny glass beads sewn –'

'Why did Nannie Burdon tell you to look for me?'

'I said, didn't I?'

'No.'

'For the biscuits. She needs a hand. I'm going to help as well. We live two doors down from her. I been cockling all morning, but Grace was my best friend before she went into service and was going to be my bridesmaid, so it's only right. And I'll be keeping the vigil with you and Nannie tonight.'

'Biscuits?'

'For Grace's funeral tomorrow. Don't you have mourners' biscuits in Middlesbrough?'

'Oh, we stopped doing that years ago. Now we have, er . . . Jaffa Cakes.'

'Sounds fancy. And what do they have at a wedding breakfast?'

Lil began to realise that her future wedding was all Martha ever thought about.

'Beans on toast,' she replied with a straight face.

'I never heard the like! What sort of beans? And what about the bride cake?'

'A pyramid of doughnuts – no one has a big wedding cake any more.'

'Never heard of that. I had my heart set on a fruit cake with two tiers, but I don't want my wedding to be out of fashion and laughed at.'

She looked so crestfallen that Lil couldn't bear to keep teasing her. She already liked this Martha.

'Fruit cake will always be best,' she assured her. 'You don't want to take any notice of silly fads. You have the wedding you want.'

Martha brightened and grinned more broadly than ever. Then she noticed the witch badge pinned to Lil's shawl.

'All the rage in Middlesbrough,' Lil explained before the question was even asked.

'See what you mean about fads,' Martha said with a laugh, and she linked her arm with Lil's.

They wended their way out of Henrietta Street and the old woman with the pipe, who was sitting nearby, peered at them through the pince-nez on her long nose. Neither Lil nor Martha had taken any notice of her; she looked like any other inhabitant of the East Cliff, wreathed in a shawl, her face hidden by the linen cap. But the woman took a small notebook from under her apron and jotted down some of the things Lil had said.

'A fantasy film?' she repeated, wondering at the peculiar-sounding phrase, then muttered a quote from *The Tempest*: '*I long to hear the story of your life, which must captivate the ear strangely.*'

Lil and Martha spent the rest of that afternoon cutting up greaseproof paper to fold into forty envelopes to put the funeral biscuits in. The biscuits themselves had been sent to Ditchburn's bakery at 95 Church Street as none of the yard cottages possessed a proper oven. Nannie Burdon had mixed the ingredients, which included caraway seeds and had been donated by every neighbour, rolled out the dough and cut it into circles which she marked by pressing an ammonite in the middle. When the envelopes were done, she produced a pencil and asked Lil to write Grace's name and age on each one, while she and Martha made sure the front room was ready to receive the night's special guest. Every speck of dust was hunted out and chased through the front door. Lil had only ever known one other person to be so house-proud and that was Verne's mother who was OCD about it. But the girl suspected everyone here in the past was the same. So much as a cobweb on view would have been the focus of gossip around the mangle. A clean step and a spotless mantelpiece were the hallmarks of respectability among the hard-working poor.

It was almost seven. Most of the menfolk had returned from work and the smells and babble of evening meals were followed by the clatter and slop of washing-up. The dried laundry had been harvested and pale purple shadows were seeping into the yard. An expectant stillness settled and people stood in their doorways, waiting. Even George remained quiet, sensing the seriousness of the occasion. Nannie Burdon lit the oil lamp.

Presently a solemn procession came through the alley. John Russell, undertaker, and his associate, both dressed like sombre crows, with tall top hats decorated with black crape, carried a coffin into the yard, led by two boys aged seven and nine.

'Nat and Frank,' Martha explained to Lil. 'Grace's brothers, right tearaways normally. They're 'prenticed in the same workshop as their dad. Where is he? He should be here to greet them.'

Nannie Burdon was quivering with barely contained rage. 'Same place he's been every free moment since his dead daughter was found. He's sat supping in the Black Horse, getting liquidated!'

Untying her apron, she bundled out of the cottage and welcomed the undertakers to the yard, directing them to her home.

Then, with a face set like that of a hanging judge,

she stomped through the alley. Her female neighbours nudged one another approvingly, while their husbands winced at what was to befall one of their own sex.

'Come in,' Martha said to the two boys. 'The table's ready for your sister to be set on.'

The undertakers entered. With professional gravity they laid the coffin down as directed. Then, to Lil's dismay, one of them unscrewed the lid and leaned it against the wall.

Nat and Frank stared at the body within. Their young faces were still covered in brown dust from the jet works and the youngest had smeared his tears and runny nose across his cheeks.

Martha gathered them to her and they clung to her skirt.

The undertakers removed their hats and bowed, absenting themselves from the cottage with the discretion of burglars. That was the signal for the other families in the yard to enter and pay their respects.

Lil avoided looking into the coffin. She didn't want to see another victim of Mister Dark; the memory of Cherry Cerise was as much as she could bear. Instead she watched the faces of the neighbours and by their reaction realised how brutal this past truly was. They were accustomed to seeing death. There wasn't one of them who hadn't endured indescribable grief. This was the next bleak panel in the grim patchwork of their lives. The wives and girls made sad-sounding noises and tucked posies beside the corpse, while the men stood gloomily by.

A kindly looking couple went up to Martha and kissed her. Even without that intimate greeting Lil would have known the girl's mother – the teeth were instantly recognisable.

Variations of 'Who could have done this terrible thing?' were on everyone's lips, and George began to sway to and fro, grumbling to himself. Finally Lil's gaze was drawn down to the coffin and she looked on Grace Pickering's face.

In the public bar of the Black Horse Hotel, the landlord, Dick Thompson, set another tankard of ale in front of Ernest Pickering.

'Knocking them back a bit swift, Ern,' Dick said, concerned.

Grace's father was hunched over. He was a big, gangly man, with brown dust on his waistcoat. Without looking up he slapped some coppers down. 'My brass not good enough?' he demanded, ending the question with the recognisable jet worker's cough.

The landlord collected the coins and said no more.

Leaning on the corner of the polished bar, and looking completely out of place in that local watering hole, wearing his smart holiday clothes,was a bulky, bearded man drinking a small glass of sherry.

Ernest Pickering could feel his deep-set eyes staring at him.

'And what might your interest be?' he snapped, not raising his gaze from the foam in his tankard. 'Not enough places on the West Cliff for you fancy folk to drink in? Or do you just enjoy peering at us poor souls over here, like so many beasts in the zoo? Why don't you throw some buns and be done?'

'That's enough now,' the landlord said sternly. 'Let the gentleman be. He's come to our town all the way from smoky old London for healthful sea air and relaxation, haven't you, sir? He doesn't want to be mithered by your vexations.'

'Ah, you would say that, Dick Thompson. You'd fill this bar with trippers and their full pockets and kick out them what live here, if you could.'

'I shall require you to leave if you carry on, Ern. It's only for your Grace's sake that I'm indulging you.'

The landlord stepped over to the tourist and apologised. 'You'll have to excuse Ernest Pickering,' he said. 'Our East Cliff manners are not so rough as a rule. The fellow's daughter is being buried tomorrow.'

'I'm sorry to hear that,' the man answered in a Dublin brogue. 'Can I buy him his next drink and shake hands? It's only good fellowship and conversation I'm after.'

'Mister,' Ernest growled, 'you'd best clear out while

you're still able. I don't like the look of you. You might be built like a brick bog, but I'm busting for a fight and I'll deck you and turn your block of a head into a bloody mash, as sure as kippers can't swim.'

'Ernest Pickering!' the landlord protested. 'You can sling yourself out of my establishment right this minute! I've had it with your boorish threats and nuisances!'

The Irish holidaymaker held up his hands. 'Let him stay,' he said. 'It's I who'll be leaving. I wouldn't come between a man and his pot o' beer at such a distressing time as this. Here's for your trouble, landlord.'

He put some coins on the bar and Dick Thompson swept them into his palm expertly, voicing his wish that the visitor return soon, before rounding on Ernest and berating him.

'Sad as I am for your loss, you're robbing me of an honest living, chasing generous patrons out of my bar. I'll ask you to grieve more cheaply.'

Ernest coughed and took a thirsty gulp of his ale.

Sitting in a corner, blending with the brown shadows, a seasoned-looking fisherman with a snowy beard on his chin and a greasy brimmed cap had watched the scene through the lenses of his pince-nez. An almost imperceptible smile lifted the corners of his mouth.

On his way out, the Irishman stood aside to permit the entry of a sharp-faced woman in a black bonnet, who glared at the interior of the inn as though she was entering a coal shed infested with cockroaches.

'I'm looking for a Mr Pickering,' she addressed the landlord. 'I've been led to believe this is where he'll be found.'

Dick didn't betray the presence of his regular customer. 'And who'll be enquiring after him?' he asked.

'My name is Axmill. I'm housekeeper over at Bagdale Old Hall, where his daughter was in service.'

The landlord's eyes slid sideways, but Ernest was already bristling and leaning back.

'I'm her dad,' he said. 'What is it you want? Can't you leave a body to mourn in peace?'

Mrs Axmill turned on her heel to view him and didn't trouble to mask the disdain that flitted across her features.

'You are Mr Ernest Pickering?' she asked.

'That's what I just said. Now state your business and go.'

'I am come at the behest of my employer, the Marquess Darqueller. On Saturday evening he sent you an epistle containing a most compassionate and philanthropic offer, but is yet to receive a reply.'

'You can tell his lordship I'm not interested.'

'What offer is this, Ern?' asked the landlord.

It was Mrs Axmill who answered. 'When he heard the distressing news, the marquess, such a large-hearted, charitable soul, was so moved that he suggested Flossy, or Grace I should say, could be interred in the new vault he has purchased for the future generations of his family. Funerals are so expensive, almost two pounds, and I understand Grace was not a member of any burial club, so that prohibitive cost will be borne by those to whom she was dearest and most beloved. Now, would such a girl as she was wish that ruinous burden to fall upon her family? Apart from the financial relief, surely any parent would be proud to have their child interred with those of noble blood?'

She reached into the black velvet purse that was dangling from her wrist and took out a folded five-pound note, which she pushed across the bar.

'I'm certain you have been put to some expense already,' she said. 'The marquess has instructed me to give you this in recompense and as a token of his deep sorrow.'

'Five whole pounds, Ern!' the landlord exclaimed. 'That's more than you've ever seen in one place.'

For some moments Mr Pickering stared at the banknote in silence. He barely took home a whole pound in wages each week. Then he raised his watery eyes at Mrs Axmill.

'*His* sorrow?' he repeated back at her. '*His* sorrow? Tell me, where was his concern when my Grace was running through the darkness in just her nightdress? What were she so scared of in your big hall that she hadn't time to put on her shoes to get away from it? The inquest didn't ask them questions, did it? How many fivers did he pay for that?'

Mrs Axmill ignored him and produced another five-pound note from the purse.

Mr Pickering took a wheezing breath. Ten pounds was a very large sum of money. Removing his hands from the tankard, he placed them flat on the bar. The left, being nearest the money, was trembling. Closing his eyes he struggled with his conscience. Then the left hand reached out.

'Just look at you, you mole grinder's sweaty backside!'

A ferocious voice rang out from the entrance. Everyone turned to see Nannie Burdon come storming in, fists and elbows flying.

'You should be ashamed, Ernest Pickering!' she cried, clumping him around the head in a violent barrage of blows that he couldn't ward off. 'The state of you, sat sitting there whilst your dead daughter is lay lying dead in my front room. I'm glad her dear mother isn't here to see this sorry day. What sort of a man are you, eh? Weak as whelk piddle, that's what you are! You're a disgrace! A lushington! You drag the whole of our yard down with you! Oh, the ignore-Minnie of it! Get gone out of here, you slobbering booze hound, and say a last goodnight to your baby girl, before the worms and crawlies get to her.'

Displaying surprising strength for her small size, she dragged him off the bar stool and continued to rain slaps and thumps upon his head as she drove him from the inn, kicking him now and then for good measure.

Mrs Axmill crumpled the five-pound notes in her hands.

'Tell me,' she said in a voice that dripped with acid, 'who was that screeching, walnut-faced fishwife and why did he let her treat him so? He stands at least three foot taller.'

'That's the Widow Burdon!' the landlord declared, as if everyone should be aware of the fact. 'No one messes with Nannie Burdon if they know what's good for them. Now, is there anything I can get you?'

'Don't be absurd,' she answered sourly, striding from the bar in a foul, thwarted temper.

In the corner, the old fisherman sipped his beer thoughtfully.

'*Good things of day begin to droop and drowse,*' he whispered, quoting from *Macbeth*. '*Whiles night's black agents to their preys do rouse.*'

4

Nannie Burdon hauled Ernest Pickering through the alley by his ear and dragged him to the wash house where she repeatedly ducked his head in a tub of cold water until he came up spluttering and somewhat sober.

'Now make yourself presentable and go kiss your Grace goodbye,' she ordered.

The man stood before her, sheepish and shamed. He swept his dripping hair back and wiped his face on his shirtsleeve. Meekly he entered her cottage.

Inside, Lil watched him approach the coffin and her heart bled for him. Though he was a tall man, he looked shrunken and beaten.

In death Grace was still beautiful, but it was a strange, unearthly beauty, like that of an immortal, untouchable statue. She didn't look as though she was simply sleeping; there was no mistaking the fact she was dead. The inner flame had been extinguished and her skin was waxy. The oil lamp above accentuated the yellowish pallor.

Her father shambled closer and he patted the coffin edge nervously, afraid to stroke her cold cheek.

'Oh, my pretty, clever Gracie,' he managed to say in a lost, despair-filled voice. 'I'm sorry I weren't there to protect you, lass. Your no-good dad let you down, like he always did. But you'll be with your mother now. She were always the best of me. She'll see you right, up there.'

A great tear ran down his nose and splashed on to the shroud. Fighting the sobs, he found the courage to lean in and kiss Grace on the forehead.

'Goodnight, God bless,' he uttered.

His knees buckled and his neighbours rushed to support him. Then he reached for his sons, and Nat and Frank led him outside like a blind man.

'Doris!' George called from the corner where he had been forgotten, causing everyone to jump.

Nannie Burdon took that as the signal to usher the families out. The vigil couldn't begin with them clogging up the place. The husbands led their reluctant wives homeward and Lil noticed that more eyes were on her than on the coffin. It was unnerving to know her mere presence was more of an unusual occurrence than an unexplained, violent death.

And so she, Martha and the current Whitby witch made themselves as comfortable as they could with a corpse in the room, and prepared to sit up all night. Nannie lit some candles and put the kettle on the hob. It was customary at these wakes for the oldest attendant to tell ghost stories, but no one was in the mood for that. Instead they chatted lightly about ordinary, day-to-day matters. Martha wanted to  know more about Lil's life in Middlesbrough, but Nannie Burdon deftly changed the subject by inquiring about wedding plans and the bride-to-be launched into a discourse about whether or not she should wear gloves, and described the handkerchief she was embroidering, adding that she would have brought it with her to work on that night, but thought it might be bad luck.

'Aye,' said Nannie Burdon, rising to fetch a small tin box from the shelf and removing a handkerchief bearing her own initials. 'I sewed this for my own bride day when I weren't much older than you. Thought I were making sensible use of my hours when I took it to a corpse waking, as there were plenty of fancy stitches to finish, even though Batty Crow told me not to. Wasn't a month after the wedding that my Jim was drowned. I'd been sewing death into my marriage, you see; don't need to be a knot witch to do that.' And she gave Lil a knowing look.

Lil said nothing. She recognised the handkerchief straightaway – it had been wrapped around the witch badge in the evil paintbox that had caused so much pain and horror in her own time.

Martha shuddered. 'Glad I didn't bring mine then!' she cried. 'My Bill's too precious. Don't know what I'd do without him. Even when we was little he kept me safe. When we was nine he thumped two bigger lads for calling me donkey face and bust one of their noses. His dad's boat'll be in tomorrow at dawn, so you'll meet him at the funeral, Lil.'

A knock at the door announced the delivery of the mourners' biscuits, by a goggle-eyed baker's boy who was desperate to see past Nannie Burdon's shoulder and get a glimpse of the corpse. It was past ten o'clock by the time the envelopes they had made were 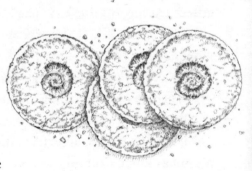 filled and sealed with blobs of black wax.

Nannie Burdon had been brewing pot after pot of her own herbal tea and fetched from the kitchen a whole Whitby gingerbread loaf, also baked at Ditchburn's. The texture was somewhere between bread and cake. It was eaten spread with butter and was delicious, better than any that Lil had eaten in the future. George enjoyed it as much as they did and was careful not to drop any crumbs.

'Read the leaves,' Martha begged Nannie. 'Tell my fortune.'

'If there's one future as doesn't need to be told in Whitby, it's yours, Martha Gales. You knows it already. You and Bill get married, and the rest of us will finally get a bit of peace from your chelp chelp chelp about that wedding.'

'Oh please! Make her, Lil. You know Nannie is gifted that way, don't you? She's got the sight – everyone round here knows it. There's even them what call her a witch.'

'Do they?' Lil uttered in mock surprise and with a smile. 'There's no such thing – and tasseomancy is daft.'

'Tassy who?' Martha asked.

'The practice of divination using tea leaves. My mum has a book on it.'

'Oh, has she?' Nannie said, slightly irked. 'Happen I'll give it a go anyway.'

She took her finest bone-china teacup and saucer with gold frilled edges from the shelf and made a fresh pot with leaves from a paper packet that she fetched from upstairs.

'Most of the enchantment lies in the tea,' she said, sticking her nose into the bag and inhaling the fragrance. 'You can't use any old leaf. I blended this from secret plants on the moor, moss that grows on gravestones, bark from haunted Mulgrave Woods, and a tiny blue flower that anchors in the cliffs and blooms only at midwinter. You have to get the measures just right, or you're like to see things no eye should witness.'

Swirling the pot around, she hummed over it, lifted the lid and whispered to the steaming infusion within. Then she poured it into the cup. The liquid was dark brown, almost black.

'Swig it down,' she told Martha. 'And wish double hard for your fate to show itself.'

'How many bairns will I be blessed with?' the girl asked, crossing her fingers then draining the cup. 'I want a dozen and the first girl I'll call Grace. How soon will Bill get his own boat? Ugh – that's a bitter brew! Is there any gingerbread left to take the taste away?'

'Now place it upside down on the saucer,' Nannie instructed. 'Close your eyes and turn it clockwise three times. Then tap it thrice, that's right – and pass it to me.'

The old woman took the cup in both hands and, holding it near a candle flame, peered inside, narrowing her eyes and pursing her lips.

'Takes an expert to read it right, mind,' she said.

'Might be a bit out of practice, but it's a knack you never lose.'

Martha clasped her hands in anticipation, but a look of sheer astonishment had stolen over Lil's face. That cup was just like the one that had belonged to her grandmother, which Jack Potts had been so charmed by. It couldn't be the exact same one, could it?

'It's all *here comes the bride* in here,' Nannie said without any surprise in her voice. 'There you are, getting hitched to the most handsome feller in the whole town.'

'Bill ain't bad looking,' the girl agreed. 'How about me? Will I look nice in my dress?'

'Show us your bloomers,' said George.

Nannie Burdon was concentrating. 'Such a frock!' she breathed. 'I never did see anything so fancy. You'll look a proper princess.'

Martha writhed with glee. 'And will we be happy forever?' she asked.

Nannie's forehead puckered. 'I can only make out the wedding,' she replied. 'It's going to be big – biggest and most important this place has ever seen.'

'Stop your teasing!' Martha said, 'Ooh, that tea is going right through. I'm going to have to pay a call again. I'm in and out that privy like a jack-in-the-box tonight!'

She took up a candlestick and hurried outside. Nannie quickly wiped the leaves from the cup with her apron, then touched her necklace. She looked flustered and troubled.

'What *did* you see in there?' Lil asked.

The old woman shook her head. 'I don't rightly know. Not seen owt like that before. I'm not exasperating when I tell you that lass's briding is going to shake the world to its roots – and I couldn't see a day beyond it. It were like . . . there weren't none to see.'

'Yes there are; I'm from way beyond it.'

'Not no more.'

Before Lil could say anything else, Martha returned.

'There's a fret come in,' she announced. 'Did you ever know a summer for so many? What do you think it means, Nannie?'

'Most times they're natural,' she answered distractedly. 'When a warm evening meets the sea's cold breath, but other times a thick haar is a purpose-drawn veil for skulking things to move about undelectable.'

'You going to have your leaves read?' Martha asked Lil. 'See if there's a champion husband out there for you?'

'I'm not looking for one! Besides, I'm only twelve! And that tea smelled *naaaasty*!'

'Every girl dreams of being a wife. At your age I'd already decided on the hymns for my day. You don't want to be an old maid.'

'Oh boy, there's so much wrong in that! I don't know where to start, so I'm going to nip to the loo as well and save an argument.'

'They have funny ways in Middlesbrough,' Martha commented when Lil had gone. 'Or was that the scarlet fever talking? Is she still a bit weak in the head from it? But what was that you were saying about a veil? Do you reckon one as long as the dress would be best? Is that what you saw in them leaves?'

Nannie Burdon chewed her lip thoughtfully as the girl nattered on.

The yard was pooled with mist that reached Lil's knees and she could see it was even thicker in the alleyway. There was no view of Church Street beyond, just a blank wall of flowing darkness. The narrow lanes of Whitby were choked with fog.

Closing the privy door behind her, Lil put the candle on the ground and hitched her skirts, gasping when she encountered the cold seat.

'I really don't want to have to get used to this,' she muttered, with a grimace. 'It's worse than that camping holiday from hell when I was ten. At least I don't need a shovel here.'

Her thoughts turned to the next day. After the funeral she would start the search for Verne, going from house to house over on the West Cliff. She had come up with the idea of making a sketch of his face by copying one of the photos in her phone and was itching to begin working on it. Taking out her mobile, she flicked through the albums and tried to choose a suitable image. Having a good drawing of her friend would be a lot easier than trying to describe him and would save so much time.

A noise directly above her head made her start. Something heavy had jumped, or landed, on the privy roof. She heard claws scratching on the fired clay tiles, followed by a low, growling mewl. Lil caught her breath.

'Catesby . . .' she mouthed.

The creature paced to and fro, the loose tiles rocking under his paws. He prowled along the row of lavatories, then returned to scrape the terracotta overhead, sharpening his talons. Did he know she was in here? Fearfully, she blew out the candle. It was too late; the beast leaped from the roof and there was a soft thump just outside the door. A waft of displaced mist blew in through the gap. Lil put both feet against the wood. A paw reached under and swiped the air angrily.

Lil flinched. She knew just how vicious this monster was, but she also realised she had to confront him, fight him off and see where he flew to. He would lead her straight to Verne. Snatching up the candlestick and gripping it like a weapon, she tapped the screen of her phone, took a deep breath and yanked the door open.

The flashlight app blasted a searing white light into the yard. Two eyes flamed brilliant green in the glare. There was a spitting hiss, an arched back, then the cat darted into the mist.

Lil slumped against the privy wall, the adrenalin leaking out of her tensed muscles. Her tightly wound dread unravelled into a fit of giggles. It had been an ordinary tabby, not Catesby at all. Switching off the light, she returned to the cottage.

Inside that snug, cosy home, Nannie Burdon had produced a couple of slender hazel twigs from somewhere and was bending them into a circle.

'Grace will need a garland tomorrow,' she explained as Lil entered. 'To hang in the church after the service and, her being a maiden, it has to be white.' Glancing up at Lil she raised her eyebrows. 'So why've you come back the colour of boiled cod?'

'A cat gave me a scare, that's all.'

The woman began sorting through a bag of cloth scraps and pulled out the whitest. 'If it were a fat ginger tom, that would be The Colonel. If it were a tabby, that's Queenie and you're lucky you had your boots on – likes to claw toes under the door does Queenie.'

'That's the one,' said Lil.

'Sodding rat chewer!' George piped up.

Nannie Burdon began cutting the fabric into

ribbons and tying them around the hoop in bows. Martha was staring into the coffin.

'Palest blue were the colour I wanted her to wear as bridesmaid,' she said sadly. 'She'd have been the fairest at my wedding, but I wouldn't grudge her that. She were a proper friend and used to help me at my lessons. I didn't find them so easy as her. Makes no sense, what's happened. She never hurt no one. Till they catch the devil what done this, none of us is safe. I'll be right glad when my Bill is back tomorrow.'

'Whitby folk used to sacrifice cats to make sure their husbands came safe home from the sea,' Nannie said. 'Didn't do nearly enough in my opinion.'

Martha's arms prickled with gooseflesh and she rubbed them, shivering.

'Someone just walked over my grave!' she exclaimed. 'Quick, Nannie, tell us a story. Nothing frightenin', not the Barguest, or the snakes, or the Old Whalers, something cheery.'

'The Old Whalers aren't nothing to be feared of,' Nannie Burdon told her. 'But I know what tale you want to hear, Martha Gales. Same one as always; been your favourite since you was four year old.'

Martha nodded and snuggled down in the corner of the settle. Lil smiled and wondered which of the town's many legends it would be. Sitting next to Martha, she unfolded a blanket and shared it with her.

'Well,' Nannie began, 'it were a long time ago

when that old goat Harry the Eight were king. It were him what smashed our fine abbey, chased out the monks and stole the gold and silver cups and plates. And as if that weren't bad enough, the greedy farthing grabber wanted to thieve our fine abbey bells and sell them for scrap, down in that London. So one fine summer day his brigands carted our beautiful ringers down the 199 steps, to the harbour, and loaded them on a ship. The people of Whitby were wailing and begging them not to rob us of them holy voices, but them hard hearted villains took no notice. As the ship set sail, the townsfolk prayed for a miracle or a vengeance on those royal pirates.'

'And the Lord heard!' Martha broke in.

'*A* lord heard,' Nannie said, but the distinction was lost on the girl. 'Though the waters were calm, that there ship began to sink, like it were a stone, and everyone on board was drowned deep, including our bells.'

'But on certain nights . . .' Martha prompted.

'On certain nights them bells can be heard tolling under the waves. And at Hallowe'en, if a man dares to stand on Black Nab rock and call his sweetheart's name, they'll peal for him, if their love is true and they're meant to marry.'

Martha sighed contentedly. 'My Bill's done that very thing,' she told Lil with pride. 'He swears he heard them and I believe him.'

Pulling the blanket up under her chin, she yawned.

'I'm never going to last till morning, I'm jiggered. Not even midnight and my eyelids are dragging.'

'I know what you need,' Nannie told her, putting the garland aside and pottering into the kitchen.

'No more tea!' Martha protested.

Nannie reappeared with a jar half full of a reddish liquid, which she poured into their cups.

'A sip of that will stop you flaggin',' she said.

Lil sniffed it cautiously. It smelled earthy and faintly of herbs and berries. It was one of Nannie's own concoctions, so she had to trust it. A moment later Lil and Martha felt like the lids of their heads had been popped open and a coal scuttle full of ice had been emptied inside. They'd never felt so wide awake.

'I calls that my Gabriel's Trumpet,' Nannie said with a chuckle. 'You could skedaddle to Robin Hood's Bay and back and not be tired now.'

'You'd make a fortune with that where I'm from,' Lil said, her senses zinging. 'Ha! Are my eyebrows standing on end? Wow! Aren't you having some?'

Nannie held up a bottle of stout and let George remove the lid with his beak. 'I'll get aquatinted with this instead,' she replied.

Lil and Martha chattered on and the clock on the mantelpiece ticked towards midnight. Nannie Burdon finished the garland, and the girls admired her work.

It reminded Lil of something her mother might sell in the family witchcraft shop. Thinking of Cassandra, she wondered if she would ever see her again. Though she had no idea what they'd say to one another if they did.

'Does Mr Pickering want some of Grace's hair?' Martha asked suddenly. 'To put in a locket or keep in his Bible?'

'Happen he will,' Nannie answered. 'And it'll be too late once she's six foot under.' She took a pair of scissors from her sewing basket and stepped across to the coffin.

Overhead, the oil lamp began to gutter.

Nannie leaned over and respectfully separated a lock of the dead girl's lustrous auburn hair.

The lamp's flame dipped, lapping feebly around the wick as it turned a cold blue. One by one the candles in the room were extinguished.

'What's going on?' Martha asked.

'Night night,' George squawked.

Nannie put the scissors to the hair, then gave a startled cry.

Grace's grey lips had parted and the corpse issued a groaning breath. Her eyes snapped open and they stared up at Nannie Burdon's face.

'By the Lords' mercy!' the old woman declared in amazement.

Martha whimpered and shrank back against the settle. Lil rose, but before she could speak a piercing squeal came from the window. Everyone turned and George began screeching. Hovering outside, flapping his leathery wings and scratching a claw down the glass like a diamond cutter, was Catesby.

Martha screamed. At the same moment the dead girl's right hand shot up and grabbed Nannie Burdon by the throat. Lil sprang to her aid, but the corpse's fingers were like a steel trap and she couldn't prise them away. Choking, Nannie sank to her knees. Maintaining that lethal grip, the body of Grace Pickering sat up in the coffin and clambered out.

Casting Nannie Burdon down it shuffled to the door, hurling the wooden chair where George was perched out of the way. The parrot shrieked and flew around the room in terror. Lil dashed to Nannie's side. The old woman was shaken and gasping for breath.

'Don't . . . don't let her out!' she croaked desperately. 'Bar the door. Pull her back!'

But the front door was wrenched open. The mist came pouring in and curled around Grace's body. Catesby mewled a command and the walking corpse followed him out into the yard.

'Stop her!' Nannie urged, struggling to her feet. 'She mustn't . . . mustn't get away!'

Lil ran after them. The fog was thicker than before – the yard was drowned in it. Grace had already disappeared, but Lil knew where she was

headed and hurried in the direction of the alley.
Stumbling through that dark, swirling tunnel she
rushed straight into a horse. The beast snorted and
tossed its great head. The one standing beside it
stamped its hooves. Both wore a plume of black
feathers in their bridles.

Lil fell back. They were harnessed to a black coach.
Between the two carriage lamps, squatting in the
coachman's seat, whip in hand, was a short, wiry
figure in a fishing gansey. Seeing Lil, Silas Gull's
sneering face twisted into a snarl and he bared his
brown teeth when her eyes met his.

'Aufwader!' she exclaimed in shock.

'Deeps damn you!' he raged, leaping up. 'Stinking landbreed with the sight. I'll lash them charmed eyes clean out of their sockets, girly!' With a yell, he swung the whip towards her. Lil ducked and felt the lash tear the air above her head.

The coach tipped. Turning, Lil saw Grace's corpse stepping inside.

'Wait!' she shouted, running to grab the small door and prevent it closing. 'You can't go!'

The door was torn from her fingers, but she stuck her head through the window and looked inside. As Grace's reanimated body sat down and leaned back against the padded leather, Lil caught sight of the person next to her. At first she thought it was a creepy life-sized doll, but it was a thin boy, dressed in a three-piece suit of blue velvet, with a white lace collar and knickerbockers, and black satin bows at his cuffs and on his shoes. In his hands he held a glittering, golden object.

'Verne!' she cried incredulously. 'Verne!'

The boy stared straight ahead as if in a trance.

'Yarr!' Silas Gull thundered, cracking the whip above the horses' ears.

The coach clattered away, the great wooden wheels rumbling over the cobbles.

'Verne!' Lil screamed, clinging to the door. 'It's me, it's Lil!'

Her best friend in the whole world took no notice. He lowered his eyes and began operating the levers and dials on the Nimius.

'Get on there, you old nags!' Silas bawled, whipping the horses faster.

The buildings of Church Street raced by. The coach rocked wildly as it plunged through the dense fog and Lil was almost thrown clear. It roared along the narrow way, rushing past the foot of the 199 steps into Henrietta Street.

'Help me!' Lil cried. 'Verne! Please! Make it stop!'

Swooping from the mist above, Catesby dived to attack. He slashed at her shoulders and lunged in to bite her neck.

Lil howled and tried to climb in through the window. But Grace Pickering raised her dead hand and gave Lil's face a violent shove. Screaming, the girl was flung from the speeding carriage.

The coach bolted on, faster and faster, hooves hammering over the ground, accompanied by Silas Gull's raucous, ugly laughter. The whip cracked again and two terrified, whinnying shrieks echoed across the fogbound headland. Then there was silence.

Face down on the cobbles, Lil groaned and raised her head. There were stinging grazes on her cheek and the palms of her hands, the back of her shirt was shredded and vicious claw marks striped her shoulder. Miraculously, no bones were broken.

'Verne!' she uttered dismally.

Staggering to her feet, she ran to the end of Henrietta Street, where it became nothing more than a grassy path. In the fog she misjudged where it ended and her foot glanced off the edge. There was no more ground in front of her, just a leap into a huge emptiness and a sheer plunge down to the shipwrecking rocks of the Scaur far below. Lil threw herself backwards and feverishly scrambled away from the brink.

When she was safe, her only thought was for the coach. Where had it gone? There was no other route, nowhere it could have veered aside to escape that drop. The harrowing truth was that those horses had galloped straight off the cliff. Even as Lil considered the chilling prospect, she knew they hadn't tumbled on to the rocks.

'The Nimius,' she breathed.

Straining her eyes, she stared out into the dark grey expanse before her. She couldn't see the West Cliff, or the harbour, and even the houses directly behind were shadowy blurs. It was as if she was standing on a tiny island, floating through oblivion. She drew a sharp breath. Was that Catesby's cry out there in the night? Yes, and there – a glimmer of light. The gleam of carriage lamps? It had to be.

'They're flying,' she whispered. 'But where to?'

Urgent footsteps behind made her spin round fearfully.

'Lil!' Martha's anxious voice called. 'That you?'

'Yes, yes, it's me.'

Martha threw her arms around Lil. 'I thought the devil himself had come and carted you off! I dashed out just in time to see that coach race into the mist, with you hanging out the window! Thought we'd lost you for always!'

Lil turned back to the blank sky, but the faint lights were gone.

'No,' she murmured, 'I'm still here. You were very brave to come after me, Martha. Thank you.'

'I already lost one friend. I weren't going to lose a new one, even though I was never so scared in all my days.' She wrapped her shawl around Lil's bare shoulder. 'So,' she said, 'I think you and Nannie have a lot to tell me, don't you? Oh, Lil, don't cry.'

5

The following morning, the funeral of Grace
Pickering went ahead as planned – or rather her
coffin, quarter-filled with sand from the beach to
make up the weight, was buried with dignified
ceremony. Nannie Burdon had insisted no one must
know what had occurred, especially Grace's father.
Who would believe them anyway?

Martha was extremely uncomfortable with the
deception, but her head was reeling from the things
she had seen and been told, and that still wasn't
everything. They had sat up until just before dawn,
explaining and discussing as much as they dared. Lil
had omitted the part about being from the future, even
though she could easily prove it with her phone. She
felt Martha was dealing with enough mind-bending
revelations already. Martha had listened attentively,
but found it difficult to grasp. She was a simple girl
and this glimpse into the sinister supernatural horrified

her. However, when Nannie and Lil had finished and she thought it over, she proved how steadfast and valuable a friend she was and promised to help Lil any way she could.

The burial took place at the Larpool Cemetery which, by then, was only thirty years old. The ancient graveyard up at St Mary's Church was full and no one had been interred there for a long time. Grace had been well liked and her father was comforted to see so many paying their last respects.

Lil didn't like the deception any more than Martha; it wasn't right, but what else could they do? She was so confused. Why did Mister Dark want Grace Pickering's corpse? What horrendous scheme was he hatching here in the past? Why was an aufwader driving the coach? But most importantly, what had Mister Dark done to Verne? Lil couldn't bear to think about how sickly and frail he looked. If only she knew where he was being kept.

She sucked the air through her teeth sharply. The wounds on her shoulder were stinging. Nannie Burdon had treated them and the grazes on her face and hands with her own ointments. The marks on the girl's cheek had almost completely faded, but the rips made by Catesby's claws would take longer to mend.

They puzzled over what their next course of action should be. Just before dawn, while they collected the coffin ballast, Nannie Burdon hid secret signs on Tate

Hill Sands, where she knew Nettie the aufwader would find them. It was their covert method of communication. Nannie could scarcely believe one of the fisherfolk was in league with Mister Dark, but Lil reminded her that he was more than an ordinary human: he was an agent of the Lords of the Deep and, with the Nimius, wielded immense power.

At the graveside, Lil took the opportunity to consider the mourners. The people from Nannie's yard she already recognised by sight, but there were others she did not. Martha was holding hands with her young man. Lil hadn't been properly introduced to Bill yet, but he was a pleasant-looking lad, albeit with serious eyes. He appeared preoccupied and had seemed distracted during the service. Lil saw Martha squeeze his hand reassuringly. It was obvious how much she adored him and Lil hoped he felt the same.

Standing apart from the group, too far away to be a part of it, yet watching keenly, was a smartly dressed man with a beard. Lil thought she recognised him from somewhere, but couldn't place it. Nearby, an old woman swaddled in a black shawl and floppy linen cap, with a bent back and a pair of gold pince-nez on her long nose, sucked on an unlit clay pipe. She too was more interested in the gathering than what the vicar was saying. Before Lil could ponder on that, her attention was diverted by a formidable stony-faced female in a dress of black taffeta, which rustled like dry leaves when she moved. Next to her was a well-padded woman who was weeping openly and blowing her flour-covered nose at regular intervals.

'From the hall, where Grace worked,' Nannie whispered, spotting Lil's curious stare. 'The tarted-up scrag-end is called Mrs Axmill – housekeeper. Always thought a mite too much of herself and now has the run of the place since the proper owners went away. Wouldn't be surprised if that frock didn't belong to her mistress. The other one is the cook, very good with pastry from what I hear, but she talks more tripe than she stews with milk and onions.'

When the coffin was lowered into the ground and handfuls of soil were cast after, Lil thought she saw a smirk steal on to Mrs Axmill's face, but she couldn't be certain.

As the mourners began to disperse, Ernest Pickering let it be known that refreshments were to be had back at his cottage, generously provided by his good neighbours, and a keg of beer had been donated by Mr Richard Thompson of the Black Horse. Nannie Burdon handed out the memoriam biscuits from a large basket and Martha brought her young man over to meet Lil.

'Here he is,' she gushed excitedly. 'My fiancé, the chap all my wedding plans are built on. If he had any sense he'd run a mile. Bill, this is Lil Burdon from Middlesbrough.'

'How do,' the young man said, shyly extending a calloused hand.

Lil shook it and gave him a friendly smile. His father's fishing coble had only returned a few hours ago and he looked dog-tired, but Bill had made a special effort to wash his neck and put on a clean shirt.

'Really nice to meet you,' Lil told him warmly. 'I've heard so much!'

'Aye, bet you have,' he said, fumbling with the peak of his cap. 'Martha has enough chat for us both.'

Martha laughed, then remembered where she was and spoke more reverentially. 'Bill's not wrong; there'll never be no want of talk in the Wilson house.'

'The . . . the what?' Lil asked, startled.

'The Wilson house. Wilson is Bill's name, didn't I say? And it'll be mine as well, soon as I says "I do".'

'Mr and Mrs Wilson?' a thunderstruck Lil uttered slowly.

'There'll be no house at all if there's more catches like what we brought in today,' Bill grumbled. 'Caught bigger tiddlers in the beck when I were a nipper. Weren't just us neither. Hardly anything for sale on Fish Pier this morning. You'd think the sea were empty. You go on to Pickering's, Martha. I got nets to tend.'

Martha followed him from the graveside. Lil stared after them, then caught Nannie Burdon watching.

'Why didn't you tell me?' the girl asked.

'Because the knowing will cast a shadow on every

choice you make now,' the old woman answered sternly. 'Even if they're not who you think they are, you'll be fretting about keeping them safe, instead of sticking to the task you came here to do.'

Lil knew she was right and the perilous complications of slipping into the past finally hit home. If Martha and Bill were her ancestors, she couldn't let either of them risk their lives. As well as rescuing Verne, she had to make sure no harm came to those two. Her own existence, and the future she had grown up in, depended on it. With a sick dread, she recalled that Nannie had been unable to see beyond their wedding in the tea leaves. Maybe there really was nothing to see.

A few hours later, in the kitchen of Bagdale Old Hall, Mrs Paddock was venting her emotions and frustrations on a ball of dough when there was an insistent knock on the door. Cursing, she clapped her hands, creating a cloud of flour, then wiped them on her apron.

'As if I didn't have enough to do, now there's just me,' she vented in exasperation. 'All right, I'm coming. Don't wear your knuckles out!'

She opened the door, expecting it to be the grocer's boy, and was primed to scold him for not turning up at the funeral that morning. He had been sweet on Grace and was always asking her to step out with him.

'So, you faithless young cabbage hound!' she declared. 'You've a nerve, showing your face here after . . .'

'Good morning, dear madam!'

Mrs Paddock brought herself up sharp. Standing before her, mid-bow, was a lively-faced middle-aged man with a merry eye and a disarming grin. His brown bowler hat had been swept off his Macassar-oiled head and his expressive eyebrows were jiggling.

'Brodribb's the name,' he announced, in a Midlands accent, eyeing her through the lenses of his pince-nez. 'Eustace Archibald Shadrack Brodribb.'

With a dramatic flourish and an expert flick of the wrist he spun the hat in the air and it landed back on his head at a rakish angle.

'Morning to you, sir,' she said. 'Though there's not much good about it.' Her hand strayed to the black armband she wore and she gave a little sniff.

'A thousand apologies and many more condolences!' he cried, whipping off the hat once more and clasping it against his chest. 'Forgive my breezy and cavalier salutation. I was ignorant of your loss. I stand before you, abject and repentant.'

'Well,' she stated, charmed by his remorse, 'that's as fulsome a sorry as I ever heard.'

His doleful face brightened.

'I name you Queen of Clemency and I am forever your humble subject, most fortunate to be in your thrall.'

'Get away now!' she said, her cheeks reddening. 'You've more sauce than a forest of ladles could manage. What's your business?'

'In a moment, dear madam. May I not first know with whom I have the delight of conversing?'

'I'm the cook,' she said, a little coyly. 'Mrs Paddock.'

'A *Mrs*! Oh, the cruelties of fate, yet what else could I expect? How I envy that most fortunate of men, your companion through life.'

'There is no Mr Paddock,' she admitted, wondering why she was being so candid with this stranger, but unable to stop herself. 'The *Mrs* is a professional title only. All cooks are a Mrs. But maybe you could call me Beatrice.'

'Ah, *Beata Beatrix*, as in the fine painting by Mr Rossetti, and the witty heroine of *Much Ado About Nothing* by Will Shakespeare. *She who makes you happy*, that's what your name means, were you aware? I'm quite certain you're the living embodiment of that definition.'

Mrs Paddock didn't know where to put herself.

She was so flustered she cupped her face in her hands and covered it in more flour than usual.

'How do you get to know so much?' she asked, marvelling.

'I'm blessed with an interested mind and a love of travel, and a trade that indulges both. I am a representative of the Entwistle and Kenyon manufacturing company and it is my honour and privilege to introduce you to the wonder of the modern mechanical age, the domestic marvel that no household should be without – the Ewbank!'

 Reaching to the side, where it had been leaning against the door frame out of sight, he produced a long handle attached to a shallow wooden box, which was fitted with rollers and brushes.

Deflated, Mrs Paddock gazed at it with disappointment.

'This dynamic miracle carpet sweeper will dispense with the need for all that laborious rug beating outdoors,' he claimed. 'Your housemaids will have so much leisure time they won't know how to fill it.'

'We don't have no maids,' she said flatly. 'We just buried our only one.'

'Oh, how obtuse of me! Yet again I crave your pardon. I don't wish to cause you any further distress. I thank you for your time on this most grievous and hot day.'

Tipping his hat, he bowed to take his leave, emitting a parched little cough as he dabbed his perspiring forehead.

'Stay a moment,' she said, taking pity on him. 'It is unpleasantly warm out there. I'm sure it's thirsty work going from door to door. I've a fresh jug of lemonade you're welcome to have a beaker of, if you'll step inside?'

The man bowed even lower and brought his Ewbank into the kitchen.

'Such a palace!' he exclaimed. 'I declare, there must be no grander environment for the preparation of fine cuisine in all of Whitby.'

'Pull up a chair,' she told him, pouring a cloudy liquid topped with slices of lemon into a glass. 'Much too big for me now, this kitchen is. Hard labour is what it is. I've only the one pair of hands. No scullery maid, no maid of any sort, no butler, just me and Jed, the groom. And the housekeeper.'

'Fallen on hard times your master, has he?'

'Bless you, no!' she said, handing him the lemonade. 'He's a marquess from some part of Prussia, where he must have his own private gold mine, if the amount he spends is anything to judge by. Never seen him in the same set of clothes twice. Likewise little Master Verne, his ward. You never saw such finery for a young lad. Proper little princeling he looks.'

'Most excellent quenching nectar,' the salesman praised, smacking his lips. 'I cannot help but wonder then, why your master doesn't appoint new staff?'

'It's not such a mystery to me. Who round here would be bold enough to work at Bagdale? Always had a reputation for being haunted, and it scared Esme off.'

'Esme?'

'She was kitchen maid. Upped and vanished without a word. At first I was led to believe it were because of a young man, but Grace didn't hold with that and now here she is, found dead in her night things by the quayside. Just what scared her so much, I ask you? There's no one in this town going to risk the same happening to them. I confess, Mr Brodribb, I'm not a woman given to fancies, but these past few nights, on my own in that attic, I'm not at ease in my bed.'

She blushed for mentioning so indelicate a subject as the place where she reposed in her nightcap.

'Esme . . .' the salesman repeated thoughtfully before blinking and pursuing the conversation. 'And you say this marquess doesn't even have a valet? That is astonishing.'

'Didn't bring no servants with him of any sort.

None of us below stairs thought it decent, but he's peculiar in his ways, eccentric you might say if you was being nicer. Oh, but he has a devil of a temper in him. A real scholar though, the hours he spends in his study, reading the medical books of Dr Power – that's the true owner of Bagdale, but he took his family and half the staff to London earlier this year. And speaking of books, the crates of them that turned up here, when the marquess took over! Now they're not cheaper by the dozen, are they?'

'What sort of books?'

'Ooh, I couldn't say. Only books I know are the ones with my recipes in, over on the dresser there. No, wait, Grace did see some once; they was even more medical and science type volumes.'

'A most learned nobleman then.'

'And I'll tell you another thing –'

'Mrs Paddock!' A stern female voice rang out.

Mrs Axmill was standing in the doorway to the servants' hall. She had changed out of her mourning gown and was now wearing a day dress of copper-coloured silk, with gigot sleeves and a tumbling abundance of creamy lace at her throat. Her suspicious glare skewered the salesman like a pin through a mounted beetle.

'And who is this person?' she demanded.

'Eustace Archibald Shadrack Brodribb,' he chirruped, jumping to his feet and touching his temple. 'Representative of the Entwistle and Kenyon manufacturing company.'

'No hawkers,' the housekeeper dismissed him with icy finality. 'Leave this property at once.'

'Oh, but Mrs Axmill!' Mrs Paddock objected. 'His handy sweeper will save so much time, if we ever get another maid.'

'I'll remind you that household affairs are my province, Mrs Paddock. These pots and pans are yours.'

'I have no wish to be the cause of an altercation,' the salesman said, taking up his Ewbank.

'Why are you still here?' Mrs Axmill asked severely.

He gave her the curtest of nods then clasped the cook's hand.

'*Fair Beatrice, I thank you for your pains,*' he said, before kissing it and striding briskly into the sunlight.

'How you demean yourself,' Mrs Axmill snorted in revulsion, gliding away into the main part of the hall.

'I know who you're saving your shrivelled mitts for,' Mrs Paddock mumbled, pulling a face and giving the dough a punishing slap. 'That's a hope without any yeast. Jed's told me the servants' gossip over at Mulgrave Castle. Your precious marquess has got his eyes set on much bigger fish than you, you scrawny scrap of broxy. What do you think he's doing there all them nights? Dinner and cards? Ho, you've a shock headed your way, Miss High and Mighty! And you look like a pantomime dame in that get-up.'

Whitby basked in the fierce sunshine and holidaymakers were out in force. The Ewbank salesman walked jauntily along Baxtergate, where he touched his hat at the ladies strolling by with their parasols, and peered into shops. Sauntering along the Golden Lion Bank, he paused to gaze in the window of Noblett's confectioner's and made a pretence of admiring the sugary treats on display.

'I do believe I could have got myself betrothed a short while ago,' he said, not even glancing at the bearded man to his left. 'If I had but pressed my amorous zeal a trifle harder, I'd never need to dine in the Beefsteak Club again.'

The burly Irishman at his side, who was wearing a pinstripe flannel suit, the sort commonly known as a 'ditto', was also affecting not to know him.

'One of these days you'll press too far and have a breach-of-promise action brought against you,' he said, seeming to address a tray of nougat through the glass. 'Was it worth the flirtation?'

'Without question. Bagdale Old Hall is undoubtedly the place. There was a servant girl called Esme who disappeared. It fits with what Grace Pickering told me the night she died.'

'Then we need to get inside that foul lair and find

some hard evidence if we're to despatch that monster.'

'The only difficulty would be getting past the housekeeper. But there may be a way . . . I wonder if a parlour maid might be found within the branches of the Brodribb family tree? Fortunately I packed a suitable wig, and the appropriate costume would be easy enough to obtain. Now, do I see myself as a Gertie or a Louisa?'

'That's a risk not worth taking. Toothless old crones are one thing, but any thing else . . . Remember what happened in Whitechapel in eighty eight when you dressed as a fallen woman. *She* spent the night behind bars, sharing a cell with three *real* doxies.'

The salesman spluttered with annoyance and rounded on the man he was supposed to be ignoring.

'I was *that* close,' he ranted, without the Midlands accent. 'That close! If it hadn't been for that imbecile of a policeman, I would have trapped the Ripper. Mary Kelly need not have died that night!'

'Sure, and if I hadn't been wasting good hours trying to get you out of gaol, *I'd* have caught that foul murderer myself. And all because you just had to knock the policeman's helmet off his oafish head.'

'It's what the character I was portraying would have done! It would not have been a sincere performance had I held back. Authenticity! How many times must I explain that to you, you pettifogging accountant!'

'O! when she's angry she is keen and shrewd,' the Irishman retaliated.

'Don't you quote The Dream at me!'

'And why not? You've not got a monopoly on the Bard!'

'Most certainly I do not, but excrutiating amateurism should always be discouraged. An averagely competent theatre manager you may be, but as an actor you stink to Zeus' throne and always have!'

They glowered at one another. It was an old resentment that would not heal. Passersby stared at them. Then the Irishman backed down and shook his head.

'We'll need to think on it some more,' he said. 'I'm sure whatever you decide will be best.'

'Naturally. Now cut along. It is almost time for Reuben Brodribb, that crusty old mariner, to settle into his corner of the Black Horse Inn.'

The men parted. The salesman raised his hat to two transfixed elderly sisters, who had watched the scene with morbid disapproval.

'If we shadows have offended,' he said, with a mischievous wink, 'think but this and all is mended, that you have but slumbered here, while these visions did appear.'

Balancing the bowler hat on top of the Ewbank's handle, he raised it aloft and spun it over everyone's heads as he disappeared into the crowd.

'We should go to Broadstairs next year, Charlotte,' one sister complained to the other, who nodded in tight-lipped agreement.

Lil Wilson walked past them. Skipping the post-funeral gathering, she had crossed the bridge, which was a completely different structure to the one she knew, to explore the West Cliff. Perhaps she would be able to spot some clue as to Verne's whereabouts. It was maddening having to wait for Nannie's aufwader friend to get in touch. Much as she was dying to meet one who wasn't brandishing a whip, she couldn't sit around idle – she had to feel as though she was actively doing something. If only her special gifts could offer any solution, but what good was knot magic here?

Martha had remained behind. Bill was being distant with her. It was unlike him and she couldn't help but worry. Lil had a sneaking suspicion she might end up in the role of relationship counsellor for her ancestors. She had tried to work out how many 'greats' ago they were and reckoned it was about four.

The West Cliff of 1890 was more genteel than in her own time. There were no shops selling novelty rock, no fish and chips or amusement arcades with flashing lights and blaring sounds. Lil missed the latter most keenly. Verne's parents owned an arcade.

She made her way to the pier and looked along the crowded beach. The bathing machines were an unexpected sight, as was the wooden stage where performers were entertaining rows of occupied deckchairs, but the carefree din of people enjoying the British seaside was exactly the same in both centuries.

Lil glanced up at the splendour of the Royal Hotel on the clifftop and was surprised to see no statue of Captain Cook, but the whalebone arch was there. Hiking up the Khyber Pass, she threaded her way through the terraced buildings until she stood before the iron gates of the Union Mill.

This close it was even more impressive and of so solid a construction it was a wonder how they would ever manage to demolish it. In spite of the stinging pain, she pulled her shawl more tightly about her shoulders; there really was a sinister feel about the place. The way the imposing central tower appeared to grow out of the wide main building was a feature she'd never seen before and all those blank windows that stared down at her made her skin creep. She was glad there was no wind, for those immense, broken sails would surely speak with many creaking, groaning voices. It was a setting that both goths and steampunkers could only dream of. Given the chance, they would flock to this grandiose edifice, which straddled both themes, to get moody photographs in their finest outfits.

'If there's anywhere in Victorian Whitby where

Mister Dark would feel at home,' she said, 'it'd have to be here.'

But there was no black coach, or stables for horses, and the huge building looked completely deserted. She could see by the undisturbed carpet of blown sand that covered the approach and courtyard that no one had set foot in there for months.

She pushed against the gate and the heavy chain that locked it rattled noisily. Turning, she wended her way back through the town and the shadow of the disused windmill crept across the road.

'Lil, hurry!' Martha called, waving her arms excitedly when she turned into Church Street. 'I've been looking for you. There's a gent here who wants to make a photograph of us in our yard. Be quick – he's setting up his funny box on legs. I never had my picture made before. Never thought I'd be in one. Think he'd do me in my wedding dress one day?'

'You and Bill OK then now?'

'I went down to the quay. He weren't wrong when he said t'other boats brought nowt back. That's never happened before. No wonder he were in such a mard. That's why we're baiting the nets early so they can go out again. Bill and his dad are getting their heads down now. T'other men have gone back to work, but with more ale inside than's wise. Grace's dad were lurchin'.'

Taking Lil's hand she pulled her through the alley.

Next to the wash house, a man in his late thirties, wearing a grey suit, with a slight professorial bearing and a luxuriant pointed beard, was adjusting one of the legs of a wooden tripod. A large, primitive camera sat on top. It was all mahogany and brass, with a black cloth draped over the back.

Four of the yard's women were sitting in front of the Gales' cottage, with a great basket of fresh mussels between them. They chatted freely as two removed the flesh from the shells and dropped it into basins, while the others mended fishing nets. They took no notice of the outlandish contraption pointing at them. The photographer was a common sight on the East Cliff and the novelty had long since evaporated for them. Nannie Burdon refused to come out of her front door. She was superstitiously wary of boxes that could capture your likeness, and didn't trust them to show the truth, so she remained by her fire, feeding George his favourite dish of cold porridge.

'Here's my friend, Mr Sutcliffe,' Martha told the photographer. 'Can she be in it as well?'

The man looked Lil up and down, like a painter appraising the suitability and possibilities of a vase in a still life. Then he pointed to the far space between the seated women. Martha pushed Lil into place and stood beside her.

Lil almost laughed. Here was the celebrated photographer, Frank Meadow Sutcliffe, about to take one of his famous photographs. Just about every home in the Whitby she knew had one of his prints on its walls. This moment was going to be frozen as the photograph that Cherry would one day show to her. She had forgotten this had to happen at some point. Grinning, Lil made sure the witch badge was clearly visible on her shawl.

'What do you do this out here for?' Martha asked him as he ducked under the cloth. 'You got a place over in Flowergate, haven't you?'

'A studio, yes,' came the muffled reply. 'But it's really only a vacant jet works, not ideal. I need larger premises.'

'But them rich folk what stay in the hotels,' Martha continued. 'They pay proper money for to have their pictures made, don't they?'

'Fortunately, yes, but not nearly enough – alas.'

'You don't sell the pictures you make of us ordinary folk though, do you?'

'No.'

'So why do it, Mr Sutcliffe?'

He reappeared from beneath the cloth. 'Sometimes I exhibit them,' he told her. 'Although that can be problematical.'

'I heard the church weren't happy with one.'

'The clergy simply doesn't understand art and what I'm trying to do. Excommunication was a ridiculous overreaction.'

'What *are* you trying to do?' Lil asked, genuinely curious. 'It's not just about the artistry is it? There's another purpose to your work, isn't there?'

He regarded her with astonishment and she wished she hadn't said anything. That wasn't something an ordinary East Cliff fishergirl would say. She really should be more guarded.

'Don't mind her, she's from Middlesbrough,' Martha explained, seeing his baffled reaction.

'No, it was an insightful question,' he said. 'And deserves a considered answer. The world we know, this world I have loved, and prize most dearly, is changing. It has become an age of steam and noise and metal wheels and pistons. This tranquil little town, this centuries-old humble way of life, will soon be washed away by the roaring tide of progress. The memory of this simple, beautiful existence will vanish and those who come after will be ignorant of how our mellow days were spent, here in the abbey's shadow.

I, in my lowly way, am endeavouring to keep a record, to preserve a shining glimpse of what was, and speak to those future generations, showing them the gentle things that have been lost. How terrible it would be if Whitby became merely a town of vanished bygones, invisible as ghosts to the grandchildren of our grandchildren. The fossils found along our coast call to us of a history long disappeared. I wish for my photographs to do the same.'

Lil longed to tell him that he succeeded and his photographs would some day be admired around the world, but she knew she mustn't. Time's secrets had to be kept, and yet she wondered how he would react if she showed him her phone and what its camera was capable of.

'How do we all squeeze inside that box to make a picture?' Martha demanded.

Mr Sutcliffe beckoned her over and allowed her to see under the cloth. Martha squealed with excitement.

'You're topsy-turvy, Lil!' she gurgled, popping out again. 'Everyone's upside down! Is that the picture made?'

'I have yet to insert and expose the glass plate,' he said, sliding a wooden cartridge into a slot and removing one side. 'The wet-collodion process captures the image in seconds. There, it's done.'

The smile had dropped from Lil's face. 'But Martha

wasn't in it!' she declared. 'Take another!'

'I don't have any more prepared plates,' he said apologetically. 'Thank you all.'

Stunned, Martha stared at him as he began packing the equipment away.

'You didn't make a picture of me?' she asked in disbelief.

'Careless, I know,' he said. 'Another time, miss.'

Martha staggered back as if he had struck her. Looking past him, she caught her reflection in one of the cottage windows.

'Donkey face,' she whispered. Covering her teeth with her hands, she fled the yard.

'Martha!' Lil cried, chasing after her. 'Come back, please!'

She caught up with her halfway up the 199 steps. The older girl was gripping the handrail and staring out across the vista of smoking chimneys.

'He didn't want me spoiling his picture,' she said through her tears, hiding her face from a well-to-do-looking family of holidaymakers who were descending the steps. 'And why would he?'

'He didn't do it on purpose,' Lil assured her, hugging her tightly. 'That didn't occur to him at all.'

'You heard him talk about beautiful things. We both know that's not me, not with these teeth that could eat an apple through iron railings.'

'Don't say that.'

'Why? That's all I've ever heard, as far back as I remember. When my Bill wasn't around to give them a hiding, the taunts never stopped and it weren't just other kids neither.'

'It doesn't matter what anyone else thinks,' Lil told her. 'You *are* beautiful, Martha.'

'Inside, you mean? Is it too wrong and bad of me to want to be pretty outside as well? Would that be too sinful a thing to wish for? It hurts, Lil. I pretend it don't, but people always stare. I hear them laugh, and the ones who think they're funny as Dan Leno ask if I want a carrot. That's a tickler, isn't it?'

'Ignore them. Bill loves you – nothing else is important.'

Martha wiped her eyes. 'He deserves better,' she said. 'What sort of a bride will I be for him? Even if I had the best frock, like Nannie said she saw in the leaves, this ugly face would still be sticking out the top of it. I know I go on and on about my wedding, but truth is that day scares me. It frights me more than all them horrors what happened last night.'

'Why? You and Bill will be so happy. It's what you always dreamed of.'

'Dreaded, you mean.'

'I don't understand.'

Martha took a gulping breath. 'What if, on my wedding, when a maiden is wearing her most prettiest dress, with her hair done nicer than it ever was, the day when she's supposed to be the most beautiful she'll ever be in her whole life . . . what if, even then, someone laughs? My poor Bill, shamed and pitied on his marriage day, and all because of . . .'

She broke down and Lil drew her close.

'That won't happen,' she promised. 'You two are going to grow old together.'

'Sometimes I want to finish with him so there'll be no wedding. If Nannie Burdon is a real witch, why can't she help me? Can't she do a spell to make me normal?'

'Oh, Martha, don't.'

'It's what I want most in the world. I'd rather die than bring shame on Bill.'

Lil pulled away and stared at her. 'Stop this,' she said sternly. 'It's not healthy. Bill is a very lucky boy, do you hear? Even so, you shouldn't let a man dictate your life. You're one of the nicest, most lovely people I know. I only met you yesterday, but now you're . . . you're like family to me.'

Martha shook her head and in a defeated voice said, 'It should have been me, not Grace, what died. He'd be so much better off if he weren't bound by his promise. Be easier for everyone: no red faces, no jeers – and no bairns cursed with my looks.'

Lil hugged her desperately again.

Three boys in sailor suits and straw hats came pushing and shoving one another down the steps.

'Hey, Neddy!' one of them called when he saw Martha. His friends began braying and they ran by, delighted with their cruelty.

'Martha,' Lil asked gently. 'I know this will sound strange, but have you, or your mum, or anyone you know . . . do you have something I could knit with?'

6

Another night of concealing mist stole over Whitby. Silas Gull had tramped halfway towards Sandsend through it, grumbling and cursing all the way. When he reached the trickle of water where Dunsley Beck flowed on to the shore, he squatted on the grassy slope and lit his pipe. A leathern flask was fastened to his belt and he gave a lusty cackle when he uncorked it. The aroma of Bagdale Hall's finest brandy tantalised his twitching nostrils and he glugged three mouthfuls before belching.

'He don't tell me when I can and can't have a snifter,' he muttered sourly. 'I'm not sitting out here all night, waiting, without a drop of tingle in my belly. Don't care what he calls himself now, he still started out as landbreed.'

The aufwader spat a glob of phlegm on the ground.

'So how long is this messenger going to take then?' he asked. 'I'm no shorewife, with nowt else to fill her time but poke about in rock pools and learn the prattle of birds.'

As he moaned to himself, a glimmer of blue light appeared on the murky horizon. When he saw it he took another swig of brandy and ground his mottled teeth. Rising off his haunches, he swaggered down the slope and crossed the shore to the fog-smothered water's edge.

The flickering beams drew closer. Silas folded his arms impatiently and sneered. It was a small wooden boat and the light was shining from a silver lantern projecting from the prow. A hunched figure wrapped in a great hooded cloak was the only occupant. The boat needed no oars: unseen forces guided and propelled it.

When it drew as close to the shore as possible, the craft came to a stop and bobbed silently on the lapping waves.

The hood turned towards him. In its deep shadow, two clustering eyes glittered.

'Silas Gull,' a whispering yet forceful voice hailed. 'I am the herald of the Deep Ones. Approach.'

The aufwader eyed it uncertainly.

'Approach.'

Muttering, Silas walked into the water until it reached his thighs and he was close to the boat.

The herald's cloak rippled as if serpents writhed and twisted beneath it.

'The skill and labour of many years have poured into the making of this deadly thing I bring thee,' the voice said. 'Every element was crafted to the intricate design of thy master, Mister Dark. The Deep Ones are highly pleased with his triumph concerning this matter. Take it now and let the circle be complete.'

There was more movement under the cloak and two pale tentacles emerged, coiled around a rectangular object wrapped in oiled cloth.

'All trace of whither it was made hath been removed,' the herald said. 'There must be no warning. Thy task is but to –'

'I know what I has to do,' Silas interrupted. 'Dark's barked it at me often enough.'

'Thou shouldst speak more softly of thy master. He is high in the Lords' favour. They wonder why he hath not yet conquered the empires of this world. They are his for the taking. No army of mankind can withstand the Nimius. Why doth he delay?'

Silas gave a dirty laugh.

'He's too busy courting,' he answered. 'There's a slippery catch he wants to land first – a fine golden fish.'

'Yet the Deep Ones are impatient to savour the destruction he will wreak across the lands.'

'Oh, they'll have their sport soon enough,' Silas promised. 'When Mister Dark is ready, every country will run a lovely sticky red. But first he wants his . . . what did he call them? His *nuptials*. He's getting wed, poor fool.'

'When is the briding to take place?'

'Tomorrow night. He wants Their blessing and begs for a sea bishop to bind it.'

'The request should come from his lips.'

'Like I said, they're busy elsewhere – har har!'

'A sea bishop shall be sent.'

'With Their full clout?'

'Representing Their might and majesty, yes.'

'Why don't you come as well? Should be a proper riot, a real shindig to remember. When were the last time you waved your tentacles?'

The boat began to drift away. It veered about and

the blue light floated into the mist.

'We shall not meet again, Silas Gull,' the herald's voice drifted back.

Silas sucked his teeth and trudged to the shore. He looked at the object he had been entrusted with and gave it an experimental shake.

'If you wish to lose your hands,' a menacing voice growled at him, 'please continue.'

Silas glanced up.

'Dark!' he exclaimed, glowering at a shadowy figure on horseback, high on the grassy ridge. 'Had to spy on me, did you? Didn't think you could trust old Silas? That's hurtful, that is.'

'Don't call me Mister Dark, you insolent animal. That name is behind me. I am the Marquess Darqueller! And I wouldn't trust you to wipe the drips off your own nose. Don't believe you're indispensable. Slime such as you is cheaply bought.'

'You doesn't want to be rid of Silas yet, your marquessness. He's the one who's going to rid you of that landmaggot with the sight I told you about. You don't want no upset so close to what you're planning, does you now?'

'You know nothing of my plans, you flap-eared cretin.'

'I made me some shrewd guesses. I'll wager they're nigh on close to the mark.'

'If I thought that, I'd cut off your repulsive head

and feed your malignant brains to Catesby. I might just do that anyway.'

Silas lowered his eyes.

'I'll deliver this,' he said. 'I know the places my Hesper stashes things in, thinking they're her own special secret, like she should have any from me. The witch hag will get your little gift tonight most like.'

'Once the circle is joined, there is no way back,' the marquess uttered with a snort. 'The power of the Lords of the Deep themselves will have sealed it. Now begone. There is other work to do this night. I've a surgery to prepare for. I hope my skills with a knife aren't rusty. I don't want the boy to die.'

Digging his spurs into the horse's sides, he galloped into the fog.

In Bagdale Old Hall, Mrs Axmill strode into the blue bedroom and turned up the gaslight. Catesby was crouched on her shoulder, his mouth red and dripping from the meat she had just fed him.

Verne Thistlewood slept soundly in the bed. A half drunk glass of milk, laced with laudanum, was on the nightstand.

The housekeeper moved closer and touched his forehead; it was clammy and cold. She lifted an eyelid with her thumb. The pupil was constricted and the boy's breathing was shallow.

'An earthquake wouldn't waken him,' she purred,

pleased with herself. 'See, Catesby, do you approve of your new abode? It won't be long now, and all those nasty headaches will cease.'

The creature shook his wings.

'You know that is not forgotten,' she reassured him. 'See . . .'

Turning the boy over, she slid a small pair of scissors from the cuff of her evening gown and snipped through the collar of his nightshirt, ripping the rest apart.

Bones were visible across the starved back. Over the surface of his skin, intricate incision guides had been drawn with ink.

'From rhomboid minor down to latissimus dorsi,' she said proudly, pointing with the scissor blade. 'Our master is growing such a magnificent new pair of wings to attach there. I will assist him in the operation. And then, my darling pet, you shall fly faster and higher than you ever have.'

Catesby leaped down to the bedpost and his eyes shone as he watched the deranged Mrs Axmill commence cutting Verne's hair down to the scalp.

'What the raging Noras have you gone and done, lady?' a fuming Nannie Burdon demanded, shaking Lil roughly.

Jolted awake, the girl opened her eyes. She was in Nannie's spare bedroom, which for many years had been used as a store for her countless jars and bottles of cures and potions. It had taken most of the previous evening just to clear a path to the bed.

When the blur of sleep had cleared, Lil saw the dumpy woman standing over her, arms folded, with a face like a smacked haddock.

'What's the matter?' she asked. 'Is something wrong?'

'Wrong, she says! Nannie cried, throwing her hands in the air in exasperation. 'How can you be lay lying there, asking that, when you know fully well the correspondable deed you done did? You'd no right to stick your hooter in where it has no business being stuck. This isn't your time, future girl! Shove your meddling in your earhole. Call yourself a witch? You don't have the sense of that birdbrain downstairs. You need to learn there are some wishes you got to walk away from.'

'Is this about Martha? I only knitted her a little scarf to wear in bed. I just wanted to help her. She was in bits yesterday.'

'Oh, was she, and did you now? Well, drag yourself out of your pit and put your head outside my door.'

Lil wrapped a shawl around her nightdress and padded downstairs.

'Gorgeous knickers!' George squawked at her.

Lil ignored him. It was very early in the morning. Over on the West Cliff the lamplighter was still dousing the street lights, but here there was a commotion out in the yard. It was thronged with people.

With a twinge of apprehension, Lil stepped outside.

Every neighbour was there and voices were raised in wonderment and admiration. Several of them were praying.

'I dunna believe it! Where'd they vanish to? It's the Queen of Sheba herself come visiting! A miracle, that's what it is. A holy blessing on our yard.'

Alarmed by those words, Lil pushed her way through. Martha was at the centre of the crowd, gasping and gurgling with joyous laughter. When her eyes lighted upon Lil she threw her arms open and rushed to embrace her.

'Oh, thank you! Thank you! Thank you!' she cried, smothering her with kisses. 'I couldn't believe it when I got up. Neither could my mam and dad. Look at them stood there, too shocked to speak. I'll never be able to repay what you did with that magic scarf. I weren't really expecting nowt to happen, but you're the best witch there's ever been!'

Lil stared at her. Martha's protruding teeth had receded overnight and she would never again be subjected to ignorant taunts and jeers – far from it. The effect this transformation had on the rest of her appearance was monumental. Her other features, which had been so eclipsed before, were now allowed to show how sublimely they were formed and aligned. Martha Gales was beautiful, not just pretty, but staggeringly lovely. Her face was achingly perfect and her new smile caused heartbeats to quicken and men to marvel.

'OMG!' Lil uttered in amazement. 'Talk about extreme makeovers. I only meant to make them less noticeable. What've I done?'

'You made my dreams come true, that's what!' Martha answered. 'If only Bill hadn't set out again. I can't wait for him to get back and see what's happened to the future Mrs Wilson.'

Drawing Lil into the centre of the crowd, she waltzed her in a circle. The neighbours began to clap in unison and even grieving Ernest Pickering joined in, beguiled by the vision of Martha's beauty. Then someone started singing a traditional song.

> *'As I was a walking on old Whitby's sand,*
> *I picked up a herring as big as my hand.*
> *Oh what do you think I made of his head?*
> *I made it into cakes and bread.'*

It was a spontaneous celebration. Eli Swales brought out his concertina and started to play, and everyone joined in the dancing and the singing.

Nannie Burdon stood in her doorway, her face grave.

'*Of all the fish that live in the sea,*' the song continued. '*The herring is the one for me.*'

Lil pulled away and dodged past the revellers.

Hugged and petted by everyone she passed, Martha followed her.

'I were going to go cockling this morning, with the other girls,' she said. 'But not now. I'll wash my hair, put on my best skirt and white stockings and take this new face for a walk. Come with me.'

'I'd love to, but I can't. I said I'd help Nannie today.'

'You can do that any time.'

'I promised. And we're still waiting for news. I watched the cliff last night, but there wasn't any sign of what you call the Old Whalers. They're our only lead to finding my friend Verne.'

Martha's attractive mouth pouted, then she shrugged. 'Well, I can't wait. I've had a lifetime of *Ee-aww*. I'm going to see what I was missing.'

She returned to the dance and Lil looked away, only to find Nannie Burdon shaking her head at her.

'Sooner you go back to where you're from, the better,' the old woman said bitterly. 'This might be the worsest bit of work you've ever done.'

Lil didn't know how to answer. She had the terrible feeling Nannie Burdon was right. Cherry Cerise would not have been proud of her.

A sensation wandered through the sunlit streets of the West Cliff that day. Martha Gales turned heads wherever she went and she lost count of the gentlemen who blundered into walls and posts because they could not wrench their eyes off her. Even ladies, from crinkle-faced fishwives to prim governesses out with their charges, admired the loveliness of this local beauty, whose looks surely stemmed from some divine source. People who would normally never look twice at her, if they even noticed her at all, were now spellbound.

Martha felt as if she was dreaming. A breathless young man jumped out in front of her, with a box of chocolates hastily purchased from Noblett's, and swore his undying devotion; another pressed a rose into her hand and ran off without uttering a word. Children called her an angel and skipped where she trod. It was an intoxicating experience. Eventually Martha espied Mr Sutcliffe, the photographer, engaged in taking a picture of three old fishermen sitting on barrels at the quayside. With a glint in her eye, she casually ambled past.

'Miss! Miss!' Mr Sutcliffe called, running after her. 'Forgive me, may I speak with you?'

The girl looked around, pretending not to know he was addressing her.

'Yes, you,' he said, catching up and gazing, enthralled, at her wide-eyed, questioning face.

'Would it be too forward of me to give you my card? Francis M. Sutcliffe. I have a studio just a stone's throw from here. I would so like to grant you immortality – please don't disappoint.'

'Immor– what?' she said, taken aback. 'That don't sound decent.'

'Oh, don't be alarmed. I assure you I intended no impropriety, I'm a happily married man. I spoke as an artist. Any painter would say the same. I have never seen so fair and pure a face as yours. It should be exalted. Poets could never do it justice, but a camera – a camera will preserve your likeness forever.'

'You want to make my picture?' Martha asked, her voice trembling.

'Very much, although I can't pay more than a few shillings if you agree.'

'You'd give me money for to do it?'

'If you would sit for me in my studio, yes. But not just there . . .'

He glanced around. Across the river, above the smoking chimneys of the East Cliff, the abbey looked like it was rearing above fermenting clouds.

'There, that would be the perfect backdrop,' he said excitedly. 'The ruins imbue the composition with a sacred, mythical quality. I see you as a physical manifestation of Whitby's spirit – a nymph born from the foaming waters, a Despoina, goddess of the Esk's mysteries. Please, pose for me, before the sun climbs too high and ruins the lighting.'

And so Martha stood by the barrels, with the rigging of the crowded harbour behind and the abbey in the distance. He gave her a fish basket to hold, emphasising her role as a child of Poseidon, and moved his camera into the best position.

Ducking under the cloth he corrected the focus and viewed the inverted scene with an appreciative eye. He would exhibit this one, perhaps even enter it in competition, and everyone would demand to know who the model was. Behind him a small crowd had gathered and murmurs of 'charming' and 'exquisite' reached Martha's overwhelmed ears.

Suddenly Mr Sutcliffe gave a shout and he shot from under the cloth as though bitten. Scuttling on his back, he hurried away from the camera and only stopped when one of the onlookers rushed over to help.

'You all right, fella?' a man asked, reaching down to calm him. 'What ails you? You're grey as a ghost and sweating like an onion. Would there be some form of battery in there. Did you get a shock? You want to be careful of electrics. My guv'nor won't have them near our theatre; it's all gas and limelight for that one.'

Breathing hard, his hands shaking, the photographer stared up at him.

'A shock? Oh yes. I thought . . . I thought.'

Mr Sutcliffe stared back at the camera and then at Martha who, like the assembled holidaymakers, didn't know what was happening.

He took out his handkerchief and wiped his forehead. The stranger helped him to his feet.

'Stupid and foolish,' he scolded himself. 'My wife is always scolding me that I work too hard. Most midnights will find me still busy in the studio, mounting the day's prints, and then I'm out at dawn to catch its ethereal qualities. Thank you, sir, I need no further assistance.'

He strode over to the camera, the hand holding the handkerchief clenched in a fist.

'Let us try that again,' he called to Martha. 'Excuse my momentary aberration, we artists are afflicted with peculiar quirks. Nothing to worry about.'

But he hesitated to look beneath the cloth once more and gestured to the man who had helped him.

'I wonder, sir,' he said. 'You have already proven yourself a Good Samaritan, but could you perform yet one more altruistic act?'

'Gladly.'

'Would you look under this cloth, at the image on the glass, and tell me what you see? Don't be confused by it being upside down – that is the way of the process.'

'I know it,' the man said. 'In my business, projected effects are often required. I've seen my share of lenses and know what tricks they can play. My guv'nor is more than glad of them, I'll tell you – and the audiences lap it up.'

'Then you're less likely to be deceived, that is excellent. If you would be so good.'

The visitor crouched down and put the cloth over

his head. Presently he emerged.

'A fine picture that will make,' he said. 'You've a grand eye.'

'It's all . . . as it should be then?'

'How would it not?'

'Yes, of course.'

Mr Sutcliffe shook himself and disappeared under the cloth. His utterance of relief was audible.

Moments later he was sliding the wooden cartridge in and exposing the glass plate.

'So,' the other man asked in a low voice, 'are you going to tell me what you thought you saw in there a few minutes ago?'

Mr Sutcliffe was reluctant to answer, but he felt churlish. This man had shown much sympathy and kindness.

'You may think me mad,' he said.

'Try me.'

'As I said, it's a lack of sleep – nothing more.'

'Go on.'

Mr Sutcliffe glanced over at Martha and squeezed his eyes shut.

'I could swear,' he said with a shudder, 'that when I looked through the lens earlier, that lovely girl was not standing there.'

'How d'you mean?'

'Something was in her place.'

'What sort of something?'

'Have you ever seen, preserved in a jar in a museum, a specimen of a large cephalopod?'

'Is it an octopus, or squid you're meaning? No, but I saw a big one washed ashore at Kilkee, County Clare ten years ago.'

'Then you know what they look like.'

'Why'd you ask?'

'Because just now, where that girl should have been, was a glistening mass of twisting, serpentine limbs.'

7

Lil spent the day helping Nannie Burdon label her huge collection of bottles and potions. They were sitting on the floor of the spare bedroom, surrounded by a multitude of dusty glass vessels. Because she couldn't read, the old woman relied on small drawings to tell her what the contents were. Unfortunately she wasn't much of an artist either and some of the symbols were a mystery to both of them.

So Lil had volunteered to write clear labels for the jars that Nannie was sure of.

'What's the use if I can't read?' Nannie had said.

'These labels aren't for you,' Lil answered. 'What if you're not well and need someone to fetch a cure? They won't find the right bottle going by your squiggly pictures.

I mean, what's this meant to be? It looks like a golf club hitting a tennis net.'

'That's spiders' webs squashed under a boot – a treatment for ague that is.'

Lil almost smiled, but what she had done to Martha still weighed heavily on her.

'What's cast is cast,' Nannie Burdon said, reading her expression. 'Us can only hope no evil will come of it.'

'I had no idea the spell would be so strong.'

'Knot magic is powerful, and you knowing what her wedded name will be, that would have made it personal. That's always dangerous, so think on.'

'Is there anything I can do?'

'Happen you and me can ask the Goddess for a blessing tonight, to watch over Martha.'

'I'd like that. I want to learn as much as I can from you while I'm here. Which might be a long time. Let's face it, I might never be going home. How can Mister Dark be hiding in a town this small?'

Nannie sucked her teeth and put her head on one side.

'Tell me about your Whitby,' she said. 'Without giving too much secrets away. Do all the kiddies there learn reading and writing? Even the girls? Poor ones as well?'

'Yes.'

'Eeh, it's a brilliant thing, to live in a world like that. That's my one big regress, not being culpable of absconding myself in the pleasure of a book. Sometimes I see the holiday folk, idling on the cliffside, faces glued to them pages, and I'm right jealous. To be sunk deep in them stories must be another kind of magic. I know I make a barmpot of myself, using words I've earwigged and don't know the meaning of. I can see folk smirking at one another – old Nannie Burdon, daft apeth, getting it wrong again. But words, to me . . . they're like feasts and I want to eat as much as I can before they're snatched away, so I guzzle and flummox myself.'

Lil smiled. 'I liked to collect old forgotten words,' she said. 'People looked at me like I was crazy if I used them. Maybe it's a witch thing.'

'Did the other witch you knew, from your time, did she like words an' all?'

'Oh yes, some of her favourites were Biba, Bowie, Hendrix and Quant.'

'Sounds like more powerful witchcraft.'

'It will be.'

Lil felt a familiar furry body lean into her leg and the happy thump of a dog's tail. Automatically she reached down to stroke the Westie's head. Then she gasped and almost burst into tears as she realised her beloved Sally had found her. The little dog's ghost rolled over for a tummy tickle and faded away.

'Wondered when that would come back,' Nannie said. 'Them first few nights when you arrived, and you was dingle-dangling by a thread, that faithful pet never left your side. Glad George couldn't see it: the language would've been worserer than usual.'

'But how did Sally get here?'

'You doesn't think there's clocks in the great behind, does you? Them we've loved aren't ruled by hours and days where they are. Makes no difference, forward or back, to them. When they want to be near, they find us.'

Lil was reassured by that.

She picked up the next jar and raised her eyebrows at the drawing. 'OK, what's this one? Looks like a potato, and – has it got legs?'

'Wart remover, what else could it be? That there's the wart, and it's running away.'

Later that day, when they were taking a break down in the front room, drinking a cup of Nannie's own reviving tea (represented by another badly drawn boot, this time kicking a bottom), Martha returned from her glorious promenading about the town. She was bursting with tales of her experiences.

'One lad swore he would pine and die for me! And Mr Sutcliffe said he's going to put my picture in his window this very evening, and everyone who walks past will see it. When I went on the beach, no one took any notice of the players on the stage there. They had to stop their songs and wait till I'd gone by, so I walked past them three times.'

'Give us a kiss,' George cried.

'I never thought I'd have such a day,' Martha breathed, her eyes sparkling.

'Aye, well, don't think you can get used to it,' Nannie told her. 'Can't spend every minute prancing up and down. There's proper graft you should have been done doing.'

Martha's lightly freckled forehead creased. 'I can't go back to mending and baiting nets,' she said. 'Gutting fish and traipsing the shore, cockling with the other girls isn't what I want to do no more.'

'Oh, and what does you want to do?' asked Nannie sharply.

Martha leaned forward. 'Mr Sutcliffe says as how he'd pay me for sitting for pictures,' she said with a heartfelt yearning in her voice. 'And he said painters would pay as well.'

'Dreams!' the old woman snorted.

'Even East Cliff girls can do that, can't they? Hopes aren't just for other folk.'

'You have to wake up sometime, and them mornings are cold and harsh.'

'Not sinful to want for better. There's a world out there I thought I'd only see in periodicals, yet a painter might want me to pose for him, in Paris maybe. What do you think, Lil?'

'There's nothing wrong in wanting change and getting on,' Lil said carefully. 'But what about Bill?

153

What would he say? And I don't think being a model is as glamorous as you think it is.'

'Bill would want me to be happy,' Martha said firmly. 'We'd just put the wedding back a year or two, till I've set enough by for him to buy a new boat.'

'If you don't talk sense,' Nannie warned her, 'I'll slap that pretty face of yours and make it cry.'

Martha struggled to hold on to her impossible fantasy a while longer, then slumped in the chair as the last shreds disappeared.

'I know,' she uttered, heaving a despondent sigh. ''Tis easy to get drunk on sugary words when you're not used to them. But it's just so much froth and bubbles, and blows away with a breath. Ah, but it were a luscious dream while it lasted.'

She inspected her hands, front and back. They were scarred from old slips with the fish and oyster knife, her nails were bitten right down and the skin was turning leathery from salt and sea and weather.

'No arty model would have rough paws like these,' she conceded. 'Unless . . . Lil, could you knit me a pair of magic mittens?'

Nannie led the laughter and George danced on the chair back – until a faint, echoing clang stilled their voices. Nannie jumped off the settle in surprise.

'So early!' she cried.

'What is it?' Lil asked, glancing out of the window.

'That weren't outside,' Martha said, turning towards

the tiny kitchen. 'It were in there, but far away.'

'Doris!' George squawked, sensing Nannie's sudden tension. 'Doris!'

The old woman looked flustered. 'You mustn't stay,' she told Martha. 'They don't like too many people about.'

'Who?' Lil asked.

'That were *them*,' Nannie explained. 'What Martha and the rest round here call the Old Whalers.'

'Aufwaders!' Lil gasped. 'But it's not dark yet!'

'They won't be coming through the streets. They was skittish enough when they carried you here and one wouldn't set foot inside at all.'

'Do they fly down the chimney?' Martha asked, staring at the fireplace in all seriousness.

'Get gone, you!' Nannie said, shooing her out. 'Your eyes can't see them no how, so don't complain.'

Martha left without further argument. 'Still,' she said before Nannie closed the door behind her, 'I done had a jamboree of a day.'

'I can stay though, yes?' asked Lil. 'I've never met one, not properly anyway.'

The old woman barred the door then drew the curtains.

'Not met proper?' she asked. 'Don't the aufwaders of your Whitby leave their caves no more? Oh, there I am, asking about what I shouldn't.'

She bustled into the kitchen and drew back the rag

rug there. Then, kneeling, she traced three spirals on a flagstone with her thumb and a silver-green light shone from the marks. There was grinding and scraping and the flagstone hinged upwards, revealing a deep tunnel cut into the earth and rock, with iron rungs set into the sheer sides.

'Even I can draw curly circles,' the old woman said when she saw the impressed look on Lil's face. 'I think it were Batty Crow who put the enchantment in this; lucky she didn't make the opening charm owt twiddly.'

'I had no idea this was here!' Lil exclaimed. 'I don't think Cherry did either. How far down does it go?'

'You'll be finding out. The aufwaders aren't coming to us, we're going to them. Fetch a light. Wish I'd got John Ditchburn to bake me a nice fresh fruit cake. That last one was a winner with them.'

She clambered down into the shaft and held her hand up to receive a lantern from Lil.

'Remember to keep your lips buttoned, 'less I tell you contrary, and don't move sudden – they're like timid mice.'

Lil waited until she had descended a little way, then lowered herself into the opening and followed.

The air that filled the narrow way was cool and smelled of soil and pitch. She hadn't gone far when she passed a bell fixed into a niche in the wall. A slender rope was attached, which trailed all the way down to the bottom.

'If it were nearer their caves it'd be heard,' Nannie's voice came up from below. 'And if it were closer to me, the whole yard would think their judgement had come.'

It wasn't much further. Soon the rungs ended and Lil found herself in a low, rocky chamber with a dry, sandy floor.

'Nannie's here,' the old woman called softly, lifting the lantern and wondering why the place was empty. 'Where you hiding and why for?'

'Hang on,' Lil said reaching into her skirt pocket. 'I've got a brighter light than that.'

Taking out her phone she switched on the flashlight.

There was a squeal and two startled, wrinkled faces were caught in the harsh white glare.

Nettie and Hesper had been watching from an opening that branched off to the left. Hesper's lifebelt

fell past her knees as she tried to run away and she fell over, losing her hat.

'Put that away!' Nannie scolded Lil. 'What did I tell you up in my kitchen? You girls have got pickled onions between your ears.'

'I'm sorry!' Lil apologised, thrusting the phone away.

'Don't go!' Nannie pleaded to the aufwaders.

Hesper had scrambled to her feet and was jamming the hat back on her head. She threw the humans a worried glance and tugged on Nettie's sleeve.

'Told you this was a bad idea,' she said. 'We must get back.'

'Wait,' Nannie begged. 'This is the girl you saved – don't be shy. You did a kind and brave deed then. She'd like to thank you.'

Nettie moved a little closer, slapping away Hesper's hands when she tried to pull her back.

'This is the girl?' Nettie ventured, staring keenly at Lil. 'Your skill is very great, Nannie. She was adrift in death's own waters when we left her in your care.'

'Just summat I had in the back of the cupboard,' Nannie said modestly. 'Her name is Lil. Don't be frighted; she's not got any more surprises in her skirt.'

The aufwaders regarded Lil warily.

'Thank you for carrying me to Nannie's cottage,' the girl said, entranced by the sight of this legendary race. 'I owe you my life.'

Nettie took a step nearer and lifted Nannie's lamp.

'The snake stones around your neck,' she said. 'A long time ago, another wore them. She was dear to us. Look, Hesper! See – our Annie is in there,

158

buried deep behind the eyes. How came this to be?'

'If Scaur Annie's in there, call her out,' Hesper insisted. 'I wants words with her.'

'Please don't,' Lil said. 'When Annie takes over, it's not easy to get rid of her again. It's a very long story.'

'I want her to know we forgave her,' Hesper said crossly.

'She knows. I promise.'

Nettie turned and peered down the dark passageway behind them.

'We must be quick,' she said. 'If we're gone too long, Tarr will wonder about Hesper and Esau's eye is always seeking me out. We shall be missed.'

Nannie cleared her throat. 'I expect you're wondering to yourselves why I asked to meet you?' she began. 'It's because –'

'You asked?' Nettie said in surprise. 'But how could you know? We only found this just before the dawn. We have had no chance to bring it to you till now. Pass the bundle, Hesper.'

Her friend hitched up her lifebelt, then handed her an object wrapped in oiled cloth.

'Didn't you see my message?' Nannie asked in disappointment.

'No. Hesper found this in one of her hoard holes.'

'Have to hide my best things from Silas, the husband,' Hesper explained. 'He'd only break them or sell them, or kill them, to spite me. I never seen this puzzler before though. I can't think who would have hid it in my best hoardy.'

'It's not ordinary, you see,' Nettie continued. 'There's a force in this. We both sense it, so we can't just leave it lying about. As it's a people thing, we felt you would know what to do?'

'Let me see,' Lil said, holding out her hands. 'I think I know what this is. In a way it's why I'm here.'

She unwrapped several layers of the cloth and revealed an all too familiar plain wooden lid. Lil despised the very touch of it.

'The paintbox,' she said with revulsion. 'Yes, this is where it starts. You have to conceal it in your kitchen, Nannie – and forget about it.'

'But how'd it get in my hoardy hole?' Hesper asked.

'I can guess who put it there. He's the reason I'm here and why we needed to see you. I don't belong to this Whitby. To me this is the past.'

'You was right, Nettie!' Hesper said.

'Let her speak,' her friend hushed.

'I came here to find a friend – my best friend in the whole world. He was kidnapped by a foul monster of a man called Mister Dark.'

'It *is* him!' Nettie cried. 'I knew that was his foul creature we've been hearing in the night.'

'Of course, you were there when he first came to Whitby,' Lil realised. 'So you know what a devil he is.

Except he's worse now, stronger – and this paintbox helped him get that way.'

'We'll do same as what we did last time,' Hesper said with a firm toss of the head. 'Run away from him. He's not our business. '

'That's where you're wrong,' Nannie told her. 'Because one of your kind is helping him.'

'That can't be,' Nettie said. 'None of the tribe would disobey our elder and have dealings with you humans.'

'Except you,' put in Hesper. 'Oh, and now me. Deeps take me – it's catching!'

'It's true,' Lil said. 'I saw him. Vicious-looking, sneery – he wanted to rip my eyes out. He called me landbreed.'

Hesper groaned and pulled the brim of her hat down over her eyes.

'So that's why he went missing,' Nettie murmured. 'And we all thought he'd had an accident and was dead.'

'Hoped he was, you mean,' Hesper muttered, still under the hat.

'You know who he is then?' Lil asked.

'Aye,' a new, angry voice called out. 'Silas Gull, my daft sister's cur of a husband.'

'Abel!' Hesper shrieked in alarm, dragging the hat off and whirling around.

Behind them a third aufwader was glowering. The intensity of his glare was alarming. Lil found she couldn't move, and neither could Nannie.

'Stop that,' Nettie told him. 'Let them go.'

He flicked his head aside and Lil felt like she had been released from a trap.

'I knew I should have brought fruit cake,' Nannie muttered by her side. Abel Shrimp was a more typical example of a male aufwader than the one Lil had seen driving the coach. Whereas Silas was wiry, hunched and sly-looking, with darting eyes and a snarling lip, Abel was lean, but straight-backed and stoic, with strong hands and a steadfastness in his bearing that compelled loyalty. His eyes were a stormy grey and his side whiskers were still predominantly sandy brown.

'What if Old Parry had followed you and not me?' he demanded of his sister. 'She'd have scarpered straight to Esau and you'd both be cast out of the tribe. What then, eh?'

'Don't blame them,' Lil implored. 'It was my fault. I needed to know where Silas would be holed up. He's got my friend.'

'I don't want to talk to you, lass,' Abel replied. 'I obey our rules, so don't you speak to me.'

Nettie had heard enough. Abel was the opposite of

Silas, but he could be extremely insufferable at times.

'If you want me to go lantern fishing with you ever again, Abel Shrimp,' she told him severely, 'you'll unstuff your gansey and show proper courtesy to this poor girl. It's that Mister Dark come back again, after all these years. Him and that winged fiend he had – and your Hesper's Silas is helping him. We have to do something.'

Abel blinked under the barrage of her words and looked uncomfortable when she finished.

'No harm meant, I'm sure,' he mumbled.

'Lad?' a voice came echoing down the passage. 'That thee, Abe, lad? What's tha doin' so far back?'

'It's Tarr!' Hesper hissed. 'Why did you bring our father here?'

'You know I didn't. I'll have to go to him.'

He gave Lil and Nannie a final look. 'I'll help you find Silas,' he said, 'but you'd best get what you need from him in the first moment, because I'm going to batter the salt clean out of his lying hide. He's had it coming a long time.'

'Lad?' the other voice called again, this time a little nearer. 'Who's thee talking to there, Abe? Thought these tunnels had been blocked up ages since.'

'You and me best go,' Abel told Hesper, and they hurried to meet their father.

Alone with the humans, Nettie gave them an encouraging smile.

'When he's not being annoying,' she said, 'there's not much wrong with Abel Shrimp. You can depend on him. He won't rest now till he's found Silas Gull.'

'Let us know right away if you can,' Lil said.

Nettie promised and melted into the shadows of the tunnel.

'George will be worrying where we went to,' Nannie said, beginning the return climb. 'Now, were it my imagination, or are Nettie and Abel sweet on each other?'

When they were back in the cottage, and George had calmed down after greeting them with a filthy rhyme, Lil put the wrapped bundle on the table and held her head in her hands.

'Still no closer to finding Verne,' she said. 'I feel so helpless. If there was just something I could do!'

'What have I got to do with this?' Nannie asked, tapping the bundle. 'You said I had to hide it?'

Lil nodded. 'There's a place in the kitchen wall, isn't there?'

'Is no secret safe from you? I'll have to find a new place for my milk stout then. Give it here.'

'Oh, wait. There's a couple of things I have to do to it, so it's the same in the future. Have you got a big piece of paper?'

Nannie Burdon went in search of the leather-bound book she pressed leaves and flowers in, that was all blank pages. While she waited, Lil removed the oiled cloth and lifted the paintbox lid.

'*Scourge Yellow*,' she said, touching the first block of pigment and recalling the suffering and death it had caused. '*Carmine Swarm . . .*'

She paused when she came to a colour that had not been inside the box when she, Verne and Cherry had found it. It was deep pink, with an image of a thorny bloom, and on the back it read *Shameless Rose*.

'What horrors are in you?' she muttered. 'I am so relieved we never found out. But I'm sure there'd have been fewer survivors at the end of it if we had.'

Removing the block, she unpinned her witch badge and, when Nannie returned with the book, asked if she might have her embroidered handkerchief.

'Be glad never to see it again,' Nannie said, taking it from the tin on the shelf.

Lil folded it around the badge and fitted them in the empty slot.

Then she tore a blank page from the book and, in large letters, wrote:

Lil Wilson, this is for you!

She stared at the words, brooding on everything that had happened and how the world she knew had been completely devastated because of this paintbox.

Underneath the message, she quickly scribbled:

Do not open it, do not use it.
Bury it again, Please!!!

If only that warning had been there, things would be so different. But she knew there was no escaping what had already happened, so she ripped the paper in two and threw the warning away.

'It's ready,' she told Nannie, after wrapping the box once more, with her message tucked into one of the layers.

Nannie Burdon carried it solemnly into the kitchen and pushed it into an alcove behind the matchboarding.

She returned to find Lil writing the names of Nannie and her two predecessors in the back of the book.

'It was the one thing left to do,' the girl explained. 'Stupid really. That was my life insurance. Until I did that, I was safe. Now I'm in as much danger as anyone else. I could die here, this minute, and the future will spin out exactly the same as it did.'

'Don't pop your clogs just yet,' Nannie told her breezily. 'I've got a lovely bit of cod for our supper.'

Martha had been unable to resist the temptation of going to see her photograph. Mr Sutcliffe had said it would be in his window by the evening, so while Nannie and Lil were meeting aufwaders, she took herself over the bridge to the West Cliff and was amazed to see a crowd gathered outside the makeshift photography studio.

'Did you ever see such sublime features?' someone was saying.

'This is as good as any daub I've seen in the Royal Academy recently.'

'The man is a genius.'

'But who is the girl? She's enchantment itself.'

Martha glowed with pride and almost walked up to them to announce her presence. Instead she gave a carefree laugh. What did she want that fantasy life for? She had a real one here, with strong roots in nourishing soil.

Without even trying to catch a glimpse of the photograph, she wrapped her shawl around her head and turned to leave.

'I beg your pardon,' a silken, cultured voice addressed her.

Martha looked up to find the most handsome man she'd ever seen smiling at her quizzically. He was resplendent in emerald-green velvet with a ruby tiepin skewering his silk cravat.

'It is you, isn't it?' he said confidently. 'The girl in

the ravishing photograph. There can be no mistaking that heavenly face.'

'Oh, sir,' she said, 'I've had enough honey poured in my ears today to last a lifetime.'

'Would champagne be preferable?'

'Sir, I realised I'm happiest with a cup of tea and a kipper. So you're wasting your breath.'

'Truly I am smitten. Mightn't I even know your name?'

'You'll be smitten good and proper if my Bill hears you talk that way.'

'Now you've ruined my stay in this charming town. All the delights have quite dissipated. I have a hated rival called Bill.'

'Get away with you,' she said, although his voice was pleasingly seductive. 'My name, if you must know it, Mr Persistent, is Martha.'

'And I, dearest Miss Martha, am the Marquess Darqueller. You are an absolute feast for the eyes, and may I be so bold as to compliment you on your neck? It really is such a pretty one.'

8

'No, Mary,' Nannie Burdon said to Martha's mother. 'We haven't seen her since late this afternoon.'

Standing on the witch's doorstep, Mary Gales wrung her hands and stared over at the alleyway, willing her daughter to come walking through it.

'Not like her,' she said. 'Never been one to go off and not tell us where. She should've been home hours ago. It's getting dark now and there's another fret creeping up from the river. My Tom is out looking. I don't like it. I can't help thinking about poor Grace. If there's a killer on the loose . . . I don't know what I'd do if . . .'

'Happen you should go to the police.'

'Tom's got no faith in the law. You saw what they was like at Grace's inquest. And nowt were done about them two Scottish girls, or the one who was killed before them. Be a different story if one of them rich holiday folk got murdered.'

She closed her eyes and took measured breaths.

'Martha were so over the moon today,' she said. 'But . . .' Leaning in, she whispered, 'I know that Lil you've got staying is a relation, so I'll not decry her, but I wish she'd left our Martha as she was. I feel it in my water she'd be home right now if she still looked the way she always did.'

'Don't give up hope just yet,' Nannie told her. 'Lil and me will go out and have a look as well.'

And so, a short while later, Nannie and Lil were walking past St Mary's Church. Night had claimed the Esk Valley and mist had rolled through the streets and lanes. Street lamps shone like amber beads on the West Cliff, and the windows of the large hotels and guest houses were similarly aglow. But the East Cliff was mostly in darkness, lit only by the waxing moon.

'Do you really think Martha is up here?' Lil asked, staring round at the huge graveyard and the black Gothic stones of the abbey.

'We're not here to look for her,' Nannie answered, marching over to the abbey cross, which was a tall, medieval pillar between the church and the ruins. The actual cross at the top had been crumbled by the elements long ago and was nothing more than a stump.

The monument stood on a wide, circular, stepped

170

base and Nannie put the basket she had brought with her on the lowest tier.

'What then?' the girl asked. 'I should be out there searching.'

'That's not helped you find your friend Verne so far, has it? Any road, did you forget we was going to ask for a blessing? That'll do more good for Martha than us rushing about like chickens.'

'Would it though?'

'No better place in all Whitby to try, this shrine being desiccated to the Goddess an' all.'

'This Christian cross?'

Nannie looked up at the weathered pillar.

'That thing?' she said with a chuckle. 'That's got nowt to do with the shrine. The cross were put up centurions later by the monks. This bit at the bottom is the shrine, didn't you know?'

'The steps?'

'Them's not steps, you backwards goose! It were a moon mirror, till they filled it in. Been a temple on this spot for . . . ooh, back when the aufwaders and us people lived side by side. There's a lot of secret powers in this town – this is one of the strongest.'

'Cherry told me Whitby is where the female energies of the universe are concentrated, or something like that. And that's why the Lords of the Deep hate us witches so much, because we protect it.'

'Happen she's right,' Nannie agreed, taking a tin bowl from her bag and pouring dried leaves and powdered tree resin into it from a jar.

'Could we get a blessing for Verne as well?'

'He's eleven, you said? If he's still more child than man, then aye. Wouldn't be worth asking if he'd swapped his toy swords for real.'

'Verne's never been like that.'

'Every man born has a seed of cruel in his heart. It's a gift from Them. Some let it flourish, others prune the hungry shoots back, but the root is always there. Now, stand next to me. Touch your necklace and bow your head. Breathe deep and welcome Her into your thoughts.'

Striking a match, she cast it into the bowl and the contents sputtered and smoked.

'Oh, Great Mother,' the witch of Whitby called. 'Hear our prayer. We beg a blessing from you. One of your daughters is lost and in need; we humbly crave your mercy and ask you to place your protection round her. You who gave life to all, watch over our friend, Martha Gales.'

The burning powder crackled and glittering silver sparks flew out. White flames erupted in the bowl and a plume of smoke rumbled upwards, forming a dense milky cloud around the stone pillar.

Lil drew away fearfully, but Nannie's hand clutched hers and pulled her back.

'Look into the smoke,' she told her. 'The Goddess has heard; this is her answer.'

The girl stared into the unnatural cloud's depths. The sparks became ancient stars burning with frosty fire, then they turned into crystal beads sewn on to an incredible gown of ivory silk. A long veil covered the wearer's head and the arms were crossed over the chest. A breath of wind lifted the veil, revealing the beautiful face beneath.

'Martha!' Lil gasped.

'The bride dress,' Nannie uttered, her eyes brimming.

The image rippled in the smoke and a dark shape began to form, closing around the ethereal figure. Lil cried out.

It was a coffin.

'She is dead then,' Nannie said, shaking her head. 'That devil got her.'

Lil wanted to turn away, but the vision was not over. The coffin began to fill with blood, and from that blood a horde of repulsive tentacles hatched. They tore through the wedding gown, and the perfect features of Martha's face bubbled and burst until only a monster of scales remained.

Lil covered her mouth. She was either going to scream or be sick.

The snake-like limbs came reaching through the smoke.

'Enough!' Nannie yelled.

A peal of thunder shook the sky and the milky cloud was empty.

'What about Verne?' Lil cried. 'Please, help me save him!'

Silence fell and the flames began to die.

'No!' Lil shouted. 'Not yet. I have to find him!'

The fire perished and the smoke blew away on the breeze.

'It's over, lass,' Nannie said sadly. 'The answer was given.'

'Like hell it is,' Lil said angrily. Whirling round, she glared at the moon. 'After everything we've done!' she bawled. 'Everything we've been through, I'm not giving up on him now. Show me!'

Nannie stared at her in astonishment and flapped her hands in consternation.

'You mustn't!' she said.

'Show Verne to me!' Lil insisted. 'Or I will not serve you. The Lords of the Deep can destroy this town and everyone in it. I don't care any more! I won't be a Whitby witch any longer!' Twisting her fingers round the ammonite necklace, she ripped it from her neck and threw it on the ground.

'Oh, Lil!' Nannie wailed.

The girl stumbled away in disgust.

'Lil!' Nannie called. 'Come back – Lil!'

Lil didn't hear her so Nannie hurried after and spun her round. 'Look!' she cried excitedly. 'The Goddess heard you. See, Lil!'

The tin bowl was blazing with new fire. Within the fierce, leaping tongues a new shape was forming. It was a frail boy lying face down on a marble slab. His head had been shaved and guide lines were inked on his scalp. Beside him was a long table where barbaric surgical instruments gleamed in readiness. The boy turned his face and opened his eyes drowsily. His lips moved and Lil heard him speak her name.

'Verne!' she wept. 'What's Dark done to you? Verne!'

A pair of giant bat wings unfurled from the flames. They stretched wide, then beat the air and the fire was extinguished.

It was over.

Lil stared in horror at the blackened tin bowl.

Lurching backwards, she gripped her head in her hands. 'Why show me that if I can't do anything to help him?' she cried. 'Where is he? Where is he?'

Nannie bowed before the shrine and put the bowl back in her basket.

'We must go home,' she said. 'I need to speak with Tom and Mary.'

Locked in their own desperate thoughts, they made their way to the 199 steps where Lil wiped her eyes.

'What did it mean?' she asked. 'That monster in the coffin – and the wedding dress?'

'I wish I knew,' Nannie answered.

'And Martha . . . poor Martha. I thought she was . . .'

'I know, but she were never your distant grandmother. Must be Bill you're descended from. This will hit him hardest. Those two were meant to be together. Happen he must wed some other lass, years from now, but Martha's shadow will lie deep over it. He'll not forget, nor stop loving her. I've seen it before.'

'It's my fault, isn't it?' Lil said, the guilt making her feel ill. 'If I hadn't turned her beautiful . . .'

Nannie uttered a cry of outrage.

'Don't you say that!' she snapped. 'A pretty face doesn't earn the evil it attracts. That's poisoned thinking. It were Mister Dark who done did this, him and no other – and Martha were always beautiful.'

Returning to the yard, Nannie took a pot from her kitchen.

'Caraway seeds for the biscuits,' she explained. 'I'll just go give them to Mary. Best you stay here.'

Leaving Lil alone with George, Nannie went to see her neighbours. There was a horrible silence, then Mary Gales' raw grief was awful to hear.

Lil retreated to the furthest corner of the room, but she didn't cover her ears. Regardless of what Nannie had said, she knew she didn't deserve to hide from the sounds of that pain.

Suddenly one of the window panes shattered. George squawked in alarm and flew to the highest shelf where he cowered behind the crockery and sent a patterned plate smashing down.

Lil flinched then ran to the door.

'Hello?' she called. Eddying mist was the only clue someone had been there.

'Doris! Doris!' the parrot screeched unhappily.

Lil coaxed him on to her hand and stroked his head until he was calm.

'I hope every neighbour doesn't do this,' she muttered as she went in search of a brush to sweep up the broken glass. Then a cry sprang from her lips.

The missile that crashed through the window had spun under the table, but it wasn't a rock as she had imagined.

'Can't be!'

It was a mobile phone.

Snatching it up, she held the phone in trembling hands. Yes, it was Verne's. Running outside, she dashed through the alley into Church Street and looked around her. There was no sign of anyone. Remembering the Nimius, she stared at the sky. Nothing.

'Why throw this?' she muttered. 'What's he trying to tell me?'

Returning through the yard, hardly daring to hope, Lil switched the phone on. There was still a charge in the battery and she went straight to his messages where she thought something might have been saved as a draft.

'No,' she murmured. 'What then? Where?'

She opened his photo album. It was filled with photos of his family, and herself. The most recent video, however, was only an hour old.

Her heart in her mouth, scared of what she might see, Lil played it.

The image was blurred and shaky and the lens was pointing away from him, showing the inside of a laboratory with large tanks of green fluid, copper pipes and polished brass gauges. Then she heard a weak, terrified voice that caused her to sink against the wall.

'Lil! It's me. It's Verne. I have to see you. Just you. They think I'm drugged, but I didn't drink it. I've got until midnight – they'll be back then. If I'm not here . . . I don't know what he'll do. He's worse than he ever was.'

The boy's voice cracked and he gulped down air, struggling to continue. Tears streaked Lil's face as she listened helplessly to his terror. The camera swung further round the laboratory. She saw a basin of surgical instruments and a tangle of discarded bandages. They were soaked with blood.

'Don't look at that,' Verne said, hastily covering the lens. 'Listen, I've found a way out. Come meet me on the West Pier. Please, Lil, please!'

The video ended, but Lil had already sped out of the cottage and was haring through the East Cliff, scything a path through the thickening sea mist. Fear and love spurred her faster than she'd ever run in her life. She bolted over the bridge and tore along the quayside, but her mind raced faster. What torture had Mister Dark inflicted on Verne? Why wouldn't he show his face? Was that his blood?

The wide stone pier was deserted.

Lil ran its length, all the way to the lighthouse. There was no sign of Verne and the stabbing pain of a stitch made her double up. High above her the harbour lantern shone out, casting its light over the fog-blanketed sea. Clutching her side, Lil turned back.

'Verne,' she breathed.

Standing at the shore end of the pier was the friend

she had journeyed back through time to save. He was dressed in a child's suit of plum-coloured velvet, with knickerbockers. The white collar was edged with lace and the cuffs were frilled. His head was swaddled in bandages.

'Verne!' she called out, hurrying towards him.

He waited for her to get closer then darted aside, to where steps led down to the beach.

'Wait!' she cried.

The boy hurried down them.

Reaching the stairs, she followed.

The beach was a blank expanse of grey fog. She could hear the waves lapping nearby, but couldn't see them. The only feature between the horizon and the cliff was the row of bathing machines.

Those wooden changing rooms, mounted on to wagons, looked sinister in the darkness. With their pitched roofs and imperfect parking, they were crowded with angles and wedges of deep black shadow. The word *ARGUMENT* was painted on their sides, after the family who owned them, with *6d for a full half-hour* in smaller italics below. They afforded plenty of cover.

'Verne?' she called uncertainly. 'You don't need to hide. Where are you?'

There was a movement ahead, behind the third bathing machine. The boy stepped out in front of it. Lil saw there was blood on the bandages.

'Oh no,' she sobbed. 'Let me help you.'

Verne climbed the machine's wooden steps. Opening the door, he went inside. Lil hurried after him. Clambering up, she entered the dark changing hut.

Verne was sitting on a stool, holding his head as if in pain. Lil wanted to rush over, but he held up his hand to keep her off.

'I've looked everywhere!' she said urgently. 'Where's he been keeping you? Verne? I can help.'

She waited for an answer, but instead he took an oil lamp from a hook and a box of matches from his pocket.

'Speak to me,' she implored. 'You said you don't have long. Why? We can get away.'

When he lit the lamp, she saw his shoulders were shaking.

'Don't cry,' she said. 'I'm here. It'll be all right now I've found you.'

'Oh, I ain't crying, you stupid pink sow,' came an ugly, muffled voice. 'I'm laughing the hairs clear out of my nose at you.'

Reaching up, he tore the bandages from his head, shaking out two large fleshy ears.

'Silas Gull!' she cried in horror.

The aufwader rounded on her and his eyes glinted. He pulled a knife from a velvet pocket and stalked towards her. Lil tried to run, but she couldn't move.

'It's what's known as the aufwader snare,' he informed her, with a lick of his teeth. 'You can't shift till I let you. Before the Deep Ones hid us from your sight, this trick served us mighty well. Been a long time since I practised it. Used to have big japes and jollies with it in the old days.'

He pressed the blade to her cheek and his foul, brandy-laced breath blew into her face.

'Your weedy pal couldn't make it, by the way,' he said. 'Nervy, ain't he? When I left, he were having a right old flap.'

Silas found this achingly funny. Then he grunted and his eyes flicked up and down.

'Skin smooth as cod roe. I could gut you right here and now, neck to belly, and you couldn't do a thing to stop me. Should I? Does you want to see how crafty I am with a cutter? Double quick that's me and Dark likes blood – him and that mangy flying mog. Even got his housekeeper drinking it now, the crab-faced old coot.'

182

He stepped away, waving the knife menacingly, letting it flash in the lamplight.

'But no. I'm too skilled in gutting. Your agony wouldn't last long, and anyone what helps one of this town's witches has earned a juicy collop of pain and fear. I got me a better idea.'

He prowled around her.

'Wanna know how you're going to die?' he asked. 'Screaming your squeaky little lungs inside out till you can't scream no more, that's how.'

He gave a filthy guffaw and Lil fell forward. The snare was lifted. Silas jumped out of the bathing machine and slammed the door. A key turned in the lock.

Throwing herself against the door, she hammered her fists on it, yelling to be let out. Then the floor tipped and pitched and she was flung down again. The oil lamp smashed and Lil was in darkness.

Outside, Silas Gull was still cackling as his aufwader strength pushed the contraption along the beach, ploughing it through the fog. The large cartwheels splashed into water and he hooted even louder.

'In you go, my lovely!' he crowed, propelling it further. 'Into the brine with you. Get your dainty toes, and everything else, good and sopping.'

Inside, Lil heard the waves sloshing beneath the planks and realised what he was doing.

'No!' she yelled, kicking the rear door, but that too was locked. Frantic, she banged the sides, but the bathing hut was sturdily built. There was a small window just under the slanting roof, but she'd never squeeze through there. Seawater began flooding in under the doors and still Silas heaved it deeper. When the wheels were almost submerged and the sea was up to his neck, he swam around and put his shoulder under the base.

'Over you go, over you go!'

The bathing machine rocked, then gave a violent lurch as he strained. Inside, Lil tumbled into the rising water, spluttering and shrieking.

'One for all witches!' Silas hollered, pushing a little higher each time. 'One for sad old Hesper and the rest of her stinking clan. And one more for the bridegroom, may he never rue the day like I did.'

With that, he gave a final upward thrust and the bathing machine toppled sideways with a tremendous splash.

Only one set of wheels showed above the fog-covered waves; the rest of the hut was submerged. Clambering up, he did a victorious jig, kicking his legs in the air. Then he stamped on the small sunken window until it broke and more water poured into Lil's death trap.

'Drown, like a rat in a box,' he cried with glee, before diving off and swimming to shore.

Moments later, exhilarated and feeling highly pleased with himself, Silas waded from the misty waves.

'Been looking for you, Gull,' a voice growled from the shadows beneath the cliff.

Silas looked up just in time to see Abel Shrimp running at him. The two aufwaders fell into the fog, throttling and punching one another. Abel was the stronger, but Silas was quicker and didn't just use his fists. He kicked and bit and his knife flashed out. He slashed his brother-in-law across the nose and sliced the top off one ear.

Abel roared and grabbed the hand that held the knife, bending it back until the wrist snapped. Silas screeched and the blade fell from his limp fingers. Then Abel's knuckles crunched into his jaw and pounded against his head. Silas was beaten; he slumped to the wet sand and Hesper's brother knelt on his chest, smashing his face with both fists.

The sea continued to gush into the bathing machine. It was up to Lil's shoulders and rising every moment. Soon she would be completely under. She screamed until it was over her chin, then started to take deep, desperate breaths. Now it was up to her nostrils. She pressed her face against the overturned side, using the last gasps of air that were left. Then the wooden hut was full.

In that cold darkness, Lil held her final breath as long as she could. Bubbles rose from her nose and she closed her eyes. She wished she had been able to rescue Verne and she hoped someone might still save him. Then she blacked out. The last thing she heard was a violent thudding.

The pitched roof of the bathing machine was being kicked off. Blow after blow rained against it, until the timber splintered and planks were prised free. Two strong arms came reaching down and hauled Lil's body out. With the waves slapping around her, she lay on the overturned hut, retching as the salt water she had swallowed and breathed in was expelled from her body.

'Reckon you'll live,' a friendly voice told her.

The girl coughed and opened her eyes. A bearded face was leaning over her. As her mind cleared, she recognised him as the Irishman from the graveyard at Grace's funeral, and somewhere else – she couldn't remember where.

'What's your name, lass?' he asked. 'Can you tell me that?'

'It's Lil,' she answered, spluttering.

'And how did you get into such a peril as that?'

'Silas!' she cried, sitting up and staring around. 'He knows where Verne is!'

On the shore, Hesper and Nettie had appeared and were now clinging to Abel's arms, dragging him away from something hidden by the fog.

'No!' Lil yelled. Leaping off the bathing machine, she tried to swim. She was a strong swimmer, but her heavy skirt dragged her under. Struggling out of it, she made it to the beach in just her petticoats.

The aufwaders stared at her in surprise. Then Nettie ran to help.

Abel gave an enraged shout and broke free from Hesper. He lunged at a figure lying in the sand.

'Stop!' Nettie shrieked. 'You've half killed him already. Do you want to finish it off and get yourself thrown out of the tribe? What would that do to your father?'

Abel lifted Silas by the throat. He raised his hand to strike again, then clenched his teeth and threw him down.

Shooting his sister and Nettie a ferocious glare, he punched the nearest bathing machine and let loose a yell of fury.

'The day is coming,' he vowed, stomping towards the steps to leave the beach, 'when that creeping worm and me will settle it once and forever, and neither of you pair will be there to stop us.'

Lil hurried to Silas and Hesper raised his head from the mist. It was a battered and bloody mess.

'He'll not tell you anything,' Nettie said gently. 'There's no waking from that beating for a few days. I'm sorry, human child.'

Lil uttered a desolate howl and fell to her knees.

'You'll catch your death out here, Miss Lil,' the Irishman declared, paddling ashore behind her. 'We both will. I was a bedridden invalid till I was seven years old. I've no desire to reacquaint myself with the condition.'

Lil glanced at the aufwaders. Nettie shook her head. The man couldn't see them. She signalled for the girl to go; they would deal with Silas.

'And these were my brand new holiday shoes,' the Irishman grumbled. 'The salt will have ruined them. Not to mention the valuables in my pockets.'

Lil turned to look up at him. She was grateful he had saved her life, but right at that moment he was getting on her nerves.

'What do you want?' she asked in exasperation.

'I'm not waiting for a thank you very kindly, if that's what you're thinking? In fact, I can chuck you back in if you'd rather? That's what I normally do with the little fishes.'

Lil realised how her behaviour must appear to him.

'I'm sorry,' she said, shivering. 'Of course I thank you.'

'Think nothing of it. But as I said, the pneumonia's no joke. I've a suite at the Royal just up there. I'm sure the wife's got something dry you could change into and we'll send you on your way.'

Lil was suddenly aware of how cold and exhausted she was.

'OK,' she agreed. 'Who are you?'

'I was christened Abraham, after my father, but I've always preferred Bram, so it's Bram Stoker . . . What's so funny?'

'There, little lady,' the Irishman said, laying a shuddering Lil on a couch in the private sitting room where he dealt with his correspondence.

The girl had collapsed on the steep climb up the Khyber Pass to the Royal Hotel, so Mr Stoker had swept her up in his arms and carried her the rest of the way. The night porter had given them a very dubious look when the red-haired giant squelched through the main entrance.

'Florence!' he called, going into another room and knocking on a door. 'Florence, will you come out? I've a girl half drowned here.'

There was a hurried, whispered discussion and presently an irritated but handsome woman came in, bearing towels, wearing a pink woollen shawl over her nightdress and her hair in a cap.

'Am I to know why I'm ministering to a freezing girl at half past one in the morning?' she asked. 'Or is this another of those sealed areas of your life I'm not to be informed of?'

'Haven't I just told you all I know? I rescued her, for heaven's sake. Or is the life of a poor fisherman's daughter not worth the saving?'

'I'm thinking if I'd married Mr Oscar Wilde, as he wished, he wouldn't be bringing girls back at all hours.'

She had been rubbing Lil's arms and legs to get the circulation going. Holding her hand, she turned it over to examine.

'Poor fisherman's daughter?' she declared, arching her brows. 'This child's never done a stroke of hard work in her life. She's got softer hands than I.'

'Is that so? How'd that be?'

'If you get a brandy for her, maybe we'll find out. And see that *you* get into some dry clothes – you're dripping on the carpet. This suite is expensive enough without having to pay dilapidations on top.'

'Right you are,' Bram said, leaving her to it.

When he returned in a fresh change of clothes, his wife had removed Lil's sopping garments and wrapped her in a huge bath towel. Lil had come round and, for a brief, snuggly moment, the comfortable room and the clean cosy towel made her think she was in her own time.

'What's on the telly?' she murmured.

'Is she all right?' Bram asked. 'She was a touch

delirious down on the beach, talking to someone who wasn't there.'

Florence took the brandy from him and put it to Lil's lips.

'If you've brought an escaped lunatic into our rooms, Abraham Stoker,' she said coldly, 'there'll be no forgiving you. There's our ten-year-old son only two rooms away – would you have him murdered in his bed?'

Tilting the glass, she poured a sip into Lil's mouth.

The girl coughed and spat it out.

'Charming,' Florence said.

'Are you back with us, Miss Lil?' her husband asked.

Wiping her lips on the towel, the girl nodded.

'I need to get back across the river,' she said. 'Can I borrow this to get there in?'

'You're not running out of here in just a towel!' Florence told her, scandalised at the notion. 'This is not Gomorrah. I will fetch something suitable.'

With a pointed look at her husband, she returned to her bedroom.

Lil gazed up at the man who had saved her. She couldn't believe it.

'You're really Bram Stoker?' she asked.

'What of it? You're sounding like you know me.'

Lil smiled to herself, but she bit her tongue. Here was someone even more famous than Frank Meadow Sutcliffe. If her mother had been here she'd have made a production number out of it and thrown her arms about his neck and clung there until crowbarred off. His writing had inspired the whole of Cassandra Wilson's life.

'So what's amused you?' he asked.

'I was thinking of my mum.'

'She a laugh a minute or something?'

'I haven't seen her for a long time.'

'Ah, that's bad. We only get the one mother. I don't see mine as often as I should. So, will you tell me now how you got yourself locked in that bathing machine? I saw it roll into the German Ocean all by itself.'

'The where? Oh, I call that the North Sea.'

'Don't change the subject. I then saw that same machine turn over as if invisible hands flipped it. What's the explanation there?'

Lil pretended not to know. She couldn't involve Bram Stoker of all people in her search for Verne.

'Here's petticoats, a skirt and a blouse.' Florence said, returning. 'I've a pair of walking boots that might fit.'

'Thank you. I'll bring them back.'

The woman looked affronted at the idea of having her charity returned – she certainly wasn't going to wear them again – but recovered quickly. 'That would be kind, yes. Now, permit her to dress in private, Bram.'

'You know more than you're cracking on,' he said to Lil as they left the room.

Lil dried herself swiftly and pulled on the clothes. They were too large, but would see her across the bridge. The boots however were a perfect fit.

As she dressed, she heard a knock at the door to the family room of the Stoker's suite.

'I've seen him, Stoker!' a voice exclaimed. 'I've seen and met our monster!'

'Quiet, please,' Florence insisted. 'Your godson has not been sleeping well in this heat – and all the strange nightly noises.'

'Fie, your pardon, dear lady,' said the newcomer, but although the voice was lowered it still had resonance.

'I had better check on him,' she said. 'If you'll excuse me?'

'I thought you'd been invited to a highfalutin party up at the castle this night?' Bram said. 'Where did you meet our devil?'

Lil couldn't help overhearing. She moved closer to the door.

'That very place! Most charming is Mulgrave

Castle, by the way. But the lawns, though pleasant, did not inspire me to dance a hornpipe like they did Dickens fifty years ago.'

'What of our monster?'

'The marquess was there to dine, same as I. He has been entertained there several evenings a week for the whole summer.'

'A fiend like that, welcomed in a big fine house?'

'It is the residence of the Marquess of Normanby. He could hardly snub one of equal rank who lived so close by, and as for our demon . . . what a charismatic play actor the brute is. I of course saw through his performance at once, but the rest of the party are not as experienced in the deceptive arts as I. They were beguiled by him and hung on his words as though they were exquisite morsels and they dogs begging for scraps.'

'You mean he upstaged you?'

'Don't be vulgar. No, the Marquess Darqueller is a most dangerous adversary and he's got his feet well under that noble table.'

'And when he visits the castle, does he leave his flying, mewling beast at home?'

'Who are you talking about?' Lil demanded, bursting into the room.

'God's eyelid!' declared a thin man in a dinner jacket, regarding her through his pince-nez. 'What ragamuffin apparition is this?'

Before Stoker could tell him, Lil demanded her answer.

'Darqueller?' she insisted. 'Is that what he's calling himself now? Where is he?'

'Was it a cattle market you were raised in?' the Irishman rebuked her. 'Where're your manners? Do you know who you're speaking to here?'

'I don't care – just tell me where Mister Dark is.'

'No idea who you're meaning, but this gentleman is none other than Henry Irving.'

The man with pince-nez gave the briefest nod; the rude girl didn't deserve more.

'You've heard of him surely?' Stoker said with a frown at her lack of reaction. 'He's only the foremost actor in the land.'

'Stoker, really,' Irving demurred with professional embarrassment. 'One can't expect recognition in the provinces, not totally anyway.'

'I don't believe there's a person in the whole country who hasn't heard of you!'

'Tell the child to avaunt. I now see the reach of our devil's ambition. It will stagger you, my friend.'

'You heard him,' Stoker told Lil. 'Get gone.'

'I'm not going anywhere,' the girl replied defiantly. 'I don't know what you two think you're doing, but you haven't a clue what you're up against.'

'Why hasn't she avaunted?' Irving asked in a stage whisper.

'You'd better put the kettle on,' Lil told them flatly. 'We've got a lot to talk about. Cats with bat wings, murdered girls drained of blood – should I go on?'

Stoker and Irving exchanged glances.

'I'll be seeing about that tea,' the Irishman murmured.

Lil told them as much as they needed to know.

'And you're certain this murderous Mister Dark of yours is one and the same as the Marquess Darqueller?' asked Mr Irving as he put his cup down, half an hour later.

'From what you've said,' Lil replied, 'I'm absolutely positive. I can't believe I didn't think to find out the name of Grace's employer sooner. It's so screamingly obvious. I would have realised straightaway. I thought Dark would be hiding in some grotty dungeon, not in plain sight in Bagdale Hall. I should have known he'd be rolling in dosh. If Verne is in there, I'm going right now.'

'Witches?' Stoker muttered in disbelief. 'Blood magic, a kidnapped child, invisible gnomey fellas under the cliff? I hope we don't look like the fools you take us for.'

'Do be quiet, Stoker,' Irving said impatiently. 'I'd have thought this was right up your street. This lurid tale sits well with your predilection for low fiction, and we've already witnessed enough damnable events to throw doubt on our established beliefs. I have not yet related the most heinous outrage the marquess is planning. Do you know who else was at the castle this night, a person who has been staying there since early summer?'

'Who?'

'Princess Maud, daughter of the Prince of Wales, granddaughter to Her Majesty Victoria. She's a most exquisite young woman, with a neck like a swan.'

'He's going to kill her,' Lil said.

'The way they were behaving throughout the evening suggests otherwise. Never have I seen so attentive a suitor and she appears totally enamoured and returns his . . . I'm loath to call them affections. It might be thought a fitting match, and high time, for the girl has been setting her tiara at Prince Francis of Teck, without the least sign of success, for far too long.'

'You think he's set on marrying her?' asked the shocked Irishman.

'That was how the wind blew – and yet I think he perceived I did not fall under his spell. I caught a flicker of doubt in his compelling eyes and he almost upset his glass.'

'It would appeal to his ego and vanity to marry into royalty,' Lil said, thinking it over. 'He started out as a manservant. Perhaps that's why he's been hanging around here. As well as being an insane killer, he's a snob. I just wish I knew the best way to fight him.'

'You?' Stoker asked with a shake of his head. 'Little girls aren't meant for facing down monsters. It's straight to bed you'll be going. If your friend Verne is in that hall, we'll rescue him.'

'Hey!' she answered hotly. 'I've seen nightmares you wouldn't believe! Skeletons flying out of graves, killer robots, gigantic insects, I've got a four-hundred-year-old dead witch sitting in my brain somewhere, so don't you tell me what monster I can't face. I've got more experience in this than two middle-aged amateurs playing detective on their holidays.'

'A very palpable hit,' Irving muttered, wincing.

Lil drained her tea, spitting out the leaves that had entered her mouth. 'And when are tea bags going to be invented?' she added crossly. It had been a long, traumatic day and she was exhausted and bad-tempered.

Florence Stoker reappeared.

'Will you lower your voices?' she scolded. 'Little Noel can hear every word. Why is this girl still here?'

'I'm just going,' Lil said, rising from her seat. 'If you guys want to come to Bagdale, fine – just don't try to stop me.'

'Fetch your pistol, Stoker,' Irving uttered.

'I jumped into the sea with it in my pocket. It's no use to man nor beast right now.'

'Then it mirrors you well, you clot. We shall have to rely solely on mine.'

'I do not want to be hearing this,' Florence declared, turning to leave the room once more.

Lil's eyes fell on her pink shawl. 'Tea bags . . .' she murmured and a wild idea blazed in her thoughts. 'Wait, can I borrow that?'

'The clothes off my very back you're wanting now?' Mrs Stoker said. 'You'll find it's warm enough out there without.'

'I don't want to wear it. I want to unravel it. Hurry up.'

Florence stared at her husband for support.

'I think the girl's in charge of this,' he said, looking uncomfortable.

The woman tightened her lips and gave Lil the shawl.

'Noel and I will be leaving tomorrow,' she said, closing a door behind her.

'I'd rather face our Bagdale devil than come back to this,' Stoker muttered semi-seriously.

'Now you two,' Lil declared with a grin on her face. 'First of all, we're going to see a witch.'

Nannie Burdon was asleep in the chair when they arrived at her cottage.

'Doris!' George squawked the moment Lil knocked on the door.

The woman jumped from the chair and let them in.

'Where did you disappear to?' she demanded. 'I thought the same happened to you as poor Martha!'

'Almost did. Silas Gull tried to drown me. This man saved my life. He's Mr Stoker and this is Mr Irving. They've been hunting Mister Dark as well. This is Nannie Burdon, wisest person in the whole of Whitby.'

Nannie thanked Mr Stoker for rescuing Lil, then peered at Irving closely.

'I know you,' she said.

'See,' Bram said proudly. 'Everyone's heard of Henry Irving.'

'Always a pleasure to meet my public,' the actor declared, bowing with a flourish.

'You're the strange fish what's been hanging about the town in silly disguises,' Nannie said. 'Now, is that your own hair or another daft wig?'

'Delightful,' Irving replied through gritted teeth.

'We know where Verne is,' Lil told her. 'He's at Bagdale.'

'So why are we dawdling? Let's get over there!'

'Surely you're not thinking of coming?' Stoker objected. 'Are we going to hire a charabanc and bring all the local old dears?'

Nannie blew a stray curl from her eyes and marched over to him, rolling up her sleeves.

'Listen, Goliath,' she warned, her nose only as high as the middle button of his waistcoat. 'You might be tall enough to be polishing my ceiling with your head, but I've felled stouter oaks than you. So just behave.'

'A doughty breed, these ladies of Whitby,' Irving observed.

Lil fetched the sewing basket.

'I've got witching of my own to do before we go,' she said. 'And we're going to need some of that Gabriel's Trumpet, if you've got any left?'

Nannie winked at her and bustled into the kitchen.

Stoker looked at Irving. 'So,' he drawled, 'this night has turned a strange corner.'

'I've a feeling it will develop a good deal further along those lines,' the actor replied.

Presently they were gathered round the table where Lil had placed a basin of water. Thanks to Nannie's energy brew, she had knitted, in record time, a small pocket out of wool unravelled from Mrs Stoker's shawl. Inside, with great solemnity, the girl placed the pigment block she had removed from the cursed paintbox and breathed deeply.

'Do we hold hands?' Stoker ventured.

'You can hold mine if you're that scared,' Nannie said, patting his.

'No, I just thought . . .'

'Do keep still,' Irving told him. 'You're fidgeting like one afflicted with St Vitus.'

'I'm just so wide awake after that juice she gave us.

I can actually feel my beard bristling. I could swim the channel or fight a hundred men.'

'One monster will be quite enough,' the actor said. 'Now, be quiet and watch. Lil's performance is about to begin.'

'OK, I've only done this once before,' the girl told them. 'I just hope it'll work as well as last time.'

'Have faith in your own gift,' Nannie encouraged her.

Lil nodded. *'Shameless Rose,'* she began, holding the knitted pocket over the basin. 'Whatever malice is within you, whatever foul plague you were created to unleash, I purge thee and transmute your power. I, Lilith Morgana Hawthorn Blossom Minerva Tempestra Wilhelmina Wilson, witch of Whitby's future, decree it and rename thee *Psychedelic Pink.'*

She plunged the pigment into the water, then stepped back and waited, breathing hard.

The colour bled through the wool and the liquid turned a muddy rose.

'What's supposed to happen?' Stoker asked.

'I'll stand on a chair and smack you round the chops if you don't shut up, big man,' Nannie threatened, slapping his hand. 'You're privy-ledged to witless a bony-fido knot witch at work. There's not many about these days you know.'

'Come on,' Lil urged, willing her magic to work. 'Come on, I need you, we all need you. Time is no barrier; Sally managed it.'

The table began to shake. The water bubbled and boiled. A pale light glimmered into existence, growing steadily brighter until it shone out, filling the room with a dazzling blast of brilliant pink. Then the opening bars of 'Ride A White Swan' by T. Rex swelled inside the cottage and Marc Bolan's voice filled their ears.

Lil hugged Nannie Burdon and the bottle witch's eyes shone with pride and amazement.

'Hello, Cherry!' Lil cried joyously.

The astounded men could only stand and gape, trying not to look afraid.

The very walls of the cottage were glowing with vibrant colour, even the flagstones and the doors. The music continued to blare and then, abruptly, it was cut off and the light died. The room seemed darker than before.

'What was that diabolic cacophony?' Irving asked.

Stoker rubbed his popping eyes and tried to shrug off his startled fear. 'That . . . that light would have come in handy for your Faust production a couple of years ago. Irving was a most marvellous Mephistopheles, you know.'

'This is more the Scottish Play,' the actor said, mopping his forehead with a handkerchief.

Lil was looking around her. 'Cherry?' she called. 'Are you here?'

'Like you couldn't get me a flamingo or a pink parrot maybe? You just ain't trying hard enough, babe,' said a glorious, familiar voice behind her. 'Strike that, *Pink Parrot* was the name of a dive I worked in once – kept getting raided and the liquor was sixty per cent Mountain Dew. Even the roaches wouldn't touch the bar snacks.'

Everyone turned.

Perched on the chair back, George was staring beadily at them. The parrot now had bright blue eyes.

'Of course I was gonna pick the most colourful thing in the room to do my party piece in,' the voice of Cherry Cerise spoke from the bird's beak. 'What did you expect? Pickin's round here are awful slim. Gotta say, I really don't love what you've done with the place.'

Lil rushed forward. 'I've missed you!' she cried.

'Good to see you too, honey. I don't wanna get overemotional, wouldn't like to poop out an egg.'

'That's a boy parrot.'

'Really? I'm not sure George knows that. You know he really wants to be called Doris, don't you?'

'That's as maybe,' Nannie remarked, folding her arms. 'But his language isn't ladylike.'

'Who's the glee club?' Cherry asked Lil.

'You don't already know?'

'Hey, gimme a break! I've been partying real hard with the most awesomest folks. My baby blues can't be everyplace at once. But I do know Dark has got our Verne. He's in a bad way, Lil. If you ain't quick, he's gonna be joining me real soon. Don't let that happen.'

Lil passed a hand over her face. Nannie Burdon squeezed her arm.

'How's it going, sister?' Cherry greeted her.

'A merry meeting to you,' said Nannie warmly.

'Oh, and this is Henry Irving and Bram Stoker,' Lil told her.

'You don't say. Well, ain't that somethin'.'

'There you go, Irving,' Bram said, nodding warily at the parrot. 'Someone's finally heard of you.'

'Would you care to explain to us mere mortals,' the actor requested, 'the reason for this music-hall turn?'

'Who stuck a popsicle between his sweet cheeks?' Cherry asked.

'Cherry is a friend of mine,' Lil said quickly, seeing him almost explode with indignation. 'She was killed by Mister Dark before he came here. She was a witch as well. We're going to need her help.'

'You don't need me, kid,' Cherry said, and the parrot moved its head from side to side. 'You've grown up real fast. You can stand on your own two feet now. You're gonna be the best witch out of all of us, and that's a hell of a long roll call. Now, go save our Verne.'

'Aye,' Stoker agreed. 'It's time we dealt with the marquess. He'll not be marrying into the royal bloodline while I've got life in my body.'

'*Here's to our enterprise!*' Irving said.

Nannie took a poker from the hearth. 'For Grace and Martha,' she said grimly.

Lil wrung her hands.

'Whatch'ya waiting for?' Cherry asked when she saw her hesitation.

'I'm scared,' the girl answered softly. 'Scared of what I'll find. The longer it's been, the worse I've felt. I failed Verne. He wouldn't have taken so long to find me. Soon as I see him, I'll know if he blames me.'

'I never heard so much baldy-rash in all my days,' Nannie said crossly. 'You've done nowt but try your best the whole time you've been here.'

'It's inaction where any failure might lie,' Bram added.

'The sun will rise in a few hours,' Irving said. 'Let us finish this righteous task together.'

Lil knew they were right. 'Bagdale then,' she said.

'Whoa!' Cherry cried. 'Where?'

'Bagdale Hall,' the girl told her. 'That's where they've got him.'

'Lil, he's not there no more.'

'What? Then where?'

'You pulling my tail feathers? It's staring you in the face.'

'What is?'

'Remember what Mister Dark does, what he is

inside. He's a master at masking, creating illusion, hiding reality.'

'I don't . . .'

'Where does your heart tell you Verne will be? When you first got here, where did you think he'd be?'

'That huge old mill? Verne's in there?'

'Go get him, babe.'

10

The towering fortress of the Union Mill was stark and black against the night sky. Standing outside the railings, the group gazed up at it.

'Been empty for years,' Stoker said. 'I've walked past this often enough, day and night and never saw so much as a mouse go in or out. Never even a candle in one of them windows.'

'Would be the perfect setting though,' Irving commented. 'Could you imagine anything more suited to be the lair of a devil such as he?'

'Doesn't matter how neglected it looks,' Lil reminded them. 'That's Mister Dark's speciality. Give me a hand getting over the fence.'

The Irishman seized her and his great arms lifted her easily over the railings.

As soon as her feet touched the ground on the other side, Lil vanished from sight.

'Hell's blazes!' he exclaimed. 'Where'd she go?

There's no star trap down there, is there?'

'I highly doubt it,' Irving told him, clambering over with as much style and dignity as he could muster. 'Nevertheless, it's pure theatre. *Lord, what fools these mortals be!*' Giving a theatrical wave, he jumped into the mill's grounds and immediately disappeared.

'There's no one can top his exits,' Bram said admiringly. 'Now, how about you, Mrs Burdon? Shall I be giving you a hoist over?'

Nannie stretched her arms out but skewered him with a warning glare.

'Just because I held your hand back in my cottage,' she said, pursing her lips prudishly, 'Don't you be getting any Balmoral ideas.'

'It's fortunate for you I'm married,' he said, heaving her up by the waist, 'or I'd be Hampton Courting you as well.'

'Oh, you saucy rogue!' she squawked, her feet kicking as she was swung over. 'It's a wallop with my poker you'll be getting.' An instant later she was gone.

Stoker rubbed his hands briskly, took a step back and vaulted the iron fence in one great bound. It was like puncturing a bubble. His ears popped and he felt tension and pressure burst around him as the barrier of concealment was breached. Everything that had been magically hidden was finally laid bare.

The Union Mill was far from derelict. It was illuminated with brilliant electric light. The five immense sails were in good repair and rotated smoothly, creating the energy that powered the hundreds of bulbs and arcing tubes both inside and out. Great quantities of overlapping, branching copper pipe encased the exterior of the tower, like metal ivy. Huge brass spheres protruded at right angles and surplus energy discharged into the air as sizzling forks of purple lightning.

'Who'd have believed that!' he cried, the words escaping his lips as soon as he landed. 'Puts to shame our mirror tricks in the Lyceum.'

'It was here all this time,' Lil murmured, staring at the incredible sight.

'I don't deserve to wear this necklace,' Nannie chided herself. 'Why couldn't I sense it?'

'You did,' Lil reminded her. 'You said you felt an evil had settled in Whitby. You just couldn't see where. You've got nothing to blame yourself for.'

Henry Irving adjusted his pince-nez and drank in the spectacle before them.

The grounds that had looked so deserted beyond the railings were crowded with innumerable empty crates, which must have contained a warehouse worth of delicate scientific instruments and machinery. Several ragged figures were shambling between the carts that still needed unloading and Nannie peered at them in surprise.

'Them's Dr Power, his family and servants!' she

declared. 'They was supposed to be in London.'

'Mister Dark's kept them as slaves,' Lil guessed. 'Even he couldn't have done all this on his own. He probably doesn't let them sleep. Look at them, they're dead on their feet.'

'There's one collapsed over there,' Stoker said. 'And another here. Poor wretches.'

'*What are these*,' Irving muttered, quoting *Macbeth* as he gazed sorrowfully at the exhausted workers. '*So wither'd and so wild in their attire, that look not like the inhabitants o' the earth, and yet are on't?*'

'This fella's been dead about a week,' Stoker said, staring down at an emaciated figure lying in the dust. 'Couldn't have eaten for at least a fortnight before that by the state of him. You wouldn't treat a mad dog so pitiless cruel.'

'This is a Godforsaken place,' Irving said.

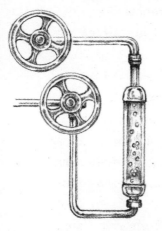

'Time we went inside,' Lil declared solemnly.

The main entrance was wide open and a pulsing green light shone within.

'Has he got a dragon in there?' Stoker mused.

The vast space inside the Union Mill was crammed with engines and vats of bubbling green acid. The very air vibrated with the thrum of the forces generated in there. Brass pressure gauges bloomed on iron partitions and jets of steam hissed out at regular intervals. Lamps of different colours flashed in sequence and sparks shot up

grilled cylinders. A noxious, acrid stench polluted the atmosphere.

Glass tanks of diverse sizes stood in rows, forming an avenue leading deeper into the building. Tubes, some connected to pumping bellows, others to reservoirs of blood and nutrients, fed into the unholy soup that filled each one, and electrodes kept the contents alive. Suspended in the cloudy fluid were repulsive shapes. Some were hybrid creatures spliced together by the surgeon's knife; others were being grown over malformed skeletons of bone and metal. All were foul and grotesque. With every fresh buzz and crackle they convulsed, or a tormented eye snapped open.

Peering into one murky tank, Nannie jumped back when two seagulls' heads smacked against the glass. They were fused to one body and the arms of a small monkey hung beneath its wings.

'*Hell is empty and all the devils are here*,' Irving said, covering his mouth with a handkerchief.

'Abominations,' Stoker uttered in disgust. 'There's not a crumb of sanity in these twitching atrocities.'

'What else would a monster create?' Lil agreed. 'Mister Dark would fill the world with horrors uglier than he is inside, if that's possible.'

'I'll wager he wouldn't stop at animals,' the Irishman added in revulsion.

Every step took them closer to the middle of the

building, directly beneath the windmill's enormous tower, where the central shaft had once turned to grind the corn. Hanging there now, in a metal cradle, to which was attached countless wires connected to the electrodes in the tanks, was the Nimius. Two of the wires trailed down to a marble slab below and Lil choked when she beheld what they were clamped on to.

In anguish, she clung to Nannie Burdon.

Upon the slab was a figure – it was Verne.

The boy lay on his stomach. His head was shaved and he wore velvet breeches but no shirt.

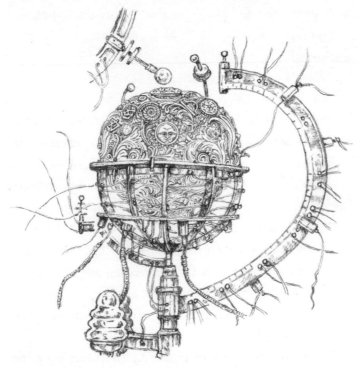

'*Angels and ministers of grace defend us,*' Irving breathed in fear.

Stoker wrenched his eyes away.

'I'm too late,' Lil cried. 'Too late!'

The wires were affixed to her friend's shoulders, to which had been grafted a pair of leathery, bat-like wings.

Tears stinging her face, Lil ran to him. The others held back, letting them have a private reunion.

Stoker nudged Irving and pointed to where two coffins were leaning against one of the control desks and, inside them, were faces that Nannie recognised.

'Grace and Martha,' she breathed. 'Curse that foul devil!'

'What's he want with them?' Stoker asked.

'Ghoulish trophies?' Irving suggested.

Both corpses were dressed in the most beautiful wedding gowns any of them had ever seen. The Marquess Darqueller had spared no expense.

Overwhelmed with love and pity, Lil approached the slab. Bandages, bottles and surgical instruments were still scattered around the floor.

'Verne,' she said tenderly. 'I'm here for you.'

The boy stirred and Lil bit her lip when she saw how starved he was. She could see every bone in his back and the angry scars where the repulsive wings had been fused to his joints and muscles.

'Lil?' his frail voice spoke. 'That you? Really you?'

'Yes, it's me, it's me. I've found you at last.'

Stroking his head, she kissed him.

'It's all going to be OK,' she promised.

He closed his eyes and sobbed. 'I tried to fight them, Lil, I really did. Dark is too strong – I've been so . . . so scared. That first night when we arrived he killed the first person we met. Ripped them to bits with his bare hands and teeth. It was . . . so much blood. He said I'd get the same if I didn't do what he said.'

'Don't think about that now.'

'I'm such a coward. Whatever he asked, I did. Then him and Mrs Axmill, they made me read a message meant for you. I'm so sorry. I knew it was a trap. I wasn't brave enough to refuse.'

Lil pressed a hand over her mouth. Was Verne really feeling guilty about that? She cast her eyes over his disfigured body and was humbled and ashamed.

'You have nothing to be sorry for,' she said through her tears. 'No one can resist Mister Dark. Remember what he did to my mother.'

Verne's eyes gazed up at her, then flicked around at the dials and gauges. A feeble smile pulled at his mouth.

'Wouldn't my dad love this place?' he said.

'Steampunk central,' she agreed, desperately battling to keep it together for his sake.

217

The boy shifted and groaned at the pain. One of the wings stretched and furled up across his legs.

'Look what they did,' he said, too sickened to glance past his shoulder. 'And there's more operations to come. They're . . . they're going to open my head.'

'We won't let them,' she said fiercely. 'We've come to get you away.'

'I don't think so,' a cold voice declared. 'Darling Catesby needs this body.'

Lil spun around and there was Mrs Axmill. The housekeeper had crept from behind a bubbling acid tank. She was dressed as a Victorian ward matron, complete with crisp starched apron and white cap tied beneath her chin. Her mouth was smeared with blood. She had been dissatisfied with the supper Mrs Paddock had prepared for her, so had decided to see if the cook tasted better than her dishes.

A revolver was in her hand and she pressed it against Lil's temple when Irving produced his small pistol.

'Throw it over there,' she told him. 'Unless you wish to see this girl's brains splattered all over her friend here.'

'You're insane, madam,' Irving said when he had done as instructed.

'*Love is merely a madness*,' she answered, smiling.

'And I love my lord more than my life and certainly more than yours, so I'm more than happy to shoot, should you give me the slightest cause.'

Gliding from the pipes overhead, Catesby alighted on Mrs Axmill's shoulder.

'And poor pusskin has such terrible headaches, you see,' she told them. 'The pressure in his stapled skull becomes too severe at times. He turns savage. That is why he needed caging. But there is so much more room in the boy's head. Catesby won't suffer those agonies any more.'

'What room?' Lil demanded, aghast.

'There'll be plenty when His Lordship removes certain unnecessary portions and fits Catesby's in their place. It will be a brand-new body for him. I'm sure he'll settle in quickly. The marquess is very much taken with the concept of minds within minds, and his other experiments are quite breathtaking, aren't they?'

'They're an abhorrence, madam,' Irving stated.

'You're mistaken. They're miracles of new life. Even the deadest heart will beat for him. I thought nothing could ever quicken in my frozen breast again, but the marquess has proved me wrong.'

'And where is your vile master?' Stoker demanded.

Mrs Axmill turned her head and strained to listen.

'There,' she said. 'Can you hear them? Difficult above the drone of the generators, but . . . there . . . yes!'

Holding his hands in the air, Stoker took several cautious paces towards the entrance.

'Is that bells?' he asked. 'At this time of night? Where are they coming from, under the cliff? There's a weird echo to them.'

Nannie Burdon touched her necklace. 'The drowned bells,' she uttered. 'The lost bells of the abbey, pealing 'neath the sea.'

As if in answer to a summons, the corpses of Grace and Martha lifted their faces and stepped out of the coffins, the trains of their exquisite gowns swishing behind them. They walked to the entrance and waited, the warm breeze wafting their veils and carefully groomed hair.

Then everyone heard the sound of horses' hooves thudding over the drive and the black carriage pulled up.

The Marquess Darqueller stepped out. He rubbed his thumb and forefinger together and sparks crackled about them. Jed the groom fell from the coachman's seat, unconscious.

Catesby rushed to greet his master, pushing the metal staples in his head against the soothing electric jags.

'Soon, my friend,' he said. 'Once the briding has taken place. I wouldn't want anything to go wrong. I still need the boy to operate the Nimius this final time.'

Opening his arms in an embrace, he approached the corpses and kissed their dead lips through the veils.

'Into the carriage, my loves,' he instructed. 'Can you hear the voices of the sunken bells? They're chiming for you. Wakening the town to witness our marriage.'

Martha and Grace obeyed. Another woman was already inside. She was out cold, in the elopement outfit the marquess had persuaded her to wear when he stole her from Mulgrave Castle two hours earlier.

Grinning, this new incarnation of Mister Dark entered the mill. Not surprised to find the others present, he smiled, then applauded Mr Irving.

'I congratulate you on your peerless ego,' he said in amusement. 'It is so inflated that even I could not overpower it over dinner. It was most disconcerting.'

The actor regarded him with loathing. 'I wish I'd put a bullet in your head then and there.'

'Not over the fish course surely? Ha, for all your conceit, you're a mean, bloodless creature, which is ironic, considering what a colossal ham you are.' He turned to Stoker. 'How do you put up with him? I hear he treats you atrociously.'

Stoker bared his teeth and his eyes burned.

'He's the best man I ever knew in my life,' he replied honestly. 'You're not fit to lick his shadow.'

'Such boyish devotion,' the marquess snorted.

Covering his mouth so no one else should see or hear, he leaned in to whisper and what he said to Stoker caused the Irishman to grab him by the throat.

'I'll see you dead!' Bram thundered.

But Darqueller was supernaturally strong. He tore Stoker's hands away and hurled him through the air. The big man spun upside down and struck a panel of knife switches and levers. Sparks flew out and he dropped to the floor. Irving ran to help him.

The marquess walked past Nannie Burdon, making a face as if he had noticed a spot of grease on his sleeve.

'These tiresome hags really do infest this town,' he groaned. 'I've already been the death of two of them, shall I make it a lucky three?'

'My witch's curse is on you,' she said simply.

'Do put the poker down, you laughable old bag.'

Moving to the marble slab, he examined Verne.

'Keep away from him,' Lil demanded. 'Haven't you done enough damage?'

'And here's another of them. Witches are like lice: just when you think you've got rid of them there's always a new infestation. How is your delicious mother, by the way? I will always be in her secret dreams, you know, tickling her in the depths of night.

I'm an itch your father will never be able to scratch. Though I think it highly unlikely you'll see either of them again.'

Lil turned away. He made her sick.

'What, no magic scarf or bedsocks today? Your knitting needles have been idle.'

Returning his attention to Verne, he lifted one of the wings and inspected the seam where the tissues met.

'They've taken well,' he said, pleased with his own skill. 'The accelerated healing is almost complete.'

Removing the wires, he instructed Catesby to fetch the Nimius from the cradle above. The creature obeyed and the marquess placed the golden device in Verne's hands.

'Get into the carriage, boy,' he said. 'You know how vital you are.'

'Where are you going with him?' Lil asked.

'He's to be pageboy. Did I not explain? This is my wedding day. You are of course all invited. The whole town will be there to witness it, even the aufwaders.'

His tone changed abruptly and he shouted at Verne to get into the carriage a second time, wrenching at his arm.

Lil snatched up a surgical knife, but Mrs Axmill knocked it from her hand and the marquess smacked the girl away. She tumbled helplessly across the floor.

Verne whimpered and crept off the slab.

'Don't hurt her,' he begged. 'I'm going. Look, I'm going.'

'Pick those wings up,' the marquess ordered when he saw them dragging behind him. Verne clenched his jaw and worked his bruised shoulder muscles. The wings lifted. They folded close to his back and he hobbled out to the waiting carriage, clutching the Nimius to his chest.

'Now, Mrs Axmill,' the marquess addressed her. 'The dowries, if you please.'

The housekeeper took a small red lacquered box from her skirt pocket and he received it with a delighted smile. Two phials of blood were inside. There was a space for one more. The woman handed him a syringe.

'What is this for?' he asked.

'My bride price,' she said, wondering why he had to ask. 'Is it not time to take it from me? And my gown. Where is it? I must make ready!'

He stared at her for several moments, then laughed.

'You surely did not think . . .? What new madness have you descended into now?'

He took a phial of blood from the pocket of his waistcoat and put it between the others.

'Whose is that?' she cried in dismay. 'I thought I was to be your third and living bride. You knew it's all I craved. Why else would I do what I've done for you? Who is she? Is she out there?'

Gun in hand, the woman stormed to the entrance and advanced towards the carriage, arm outstretched, her finger on the trigger.

Darqueller caught her. Grabbing her wrist, he twisted it around and pulled her face close to his, as if for a tender kiss. A shot rang out and Mrs Axmill fell at his feet.

Without another glance at the mill, he climbed into the coachman's seat and whipped the horses. The hour he had long awaited was finally here.

Catesby left his shoulder and lingered in the grounds. When he had eaten as much of the housekeeper as he wished, he took to the air and followed the wedding party.

The music of the drowned bells echoed through the ancient stones of Whitby and the whole town was placed under a profound enchantment. The inhabitants left their beds, trailing down to the quayside where they waited and turned their faces to the harbour mouth. The great doors leading to the aufwader caves swung open in the rocky cliff and the fisherfolk answered the call. They clambered on to the East Pier and bowed their heads in reverence. Abel slipped his bruised hand into Nettie's and she gripped it anxiously. Hesper put her arm through that of her father, and

Tarr leaned more heavily on his stick than he ever had.

Darkness still prevailed, though on the horizon there was a dim blur of pale light between sea and sky. Grey mist covered the waters, but shapes began leaping through. Seals barked as they swam up the river, then came the porpoises, followed by a pod of humpback whales. Sea birds wheeled overhead in vast numbers until they settled on every rooftop. Crustaceans of all shapes and sizes, some never seen before, crawled up the harbour walls and over the hulls of fishing vessels. Then a calm rippled over the expectant town and only the bells could be heard.

The Marquess Darqueller drove the carriage down the narrow streets with a callous disregard for the lives of people in his way. Reining the horses by the bridge, he dismounted and opened the carriage door.

Grace and Martha stepped down, their veils billowing around them like two white flames as they took their places on the bridge.

Darqueller reached into the carriage and lifted out a slender woman in a gown of purple silk. It was the Princess Maud of Wales. Gazing around him, he grinned and carried the unconscious princess to where the dead girls were waiting. He called for Verne to follow.

Still holding the Nimius, the boy emerged. His wings fanned open as the breeze caught them and Verne halted. It felt good. He stretched his back and they extended to their full span. They were as wide as the bridge itself.

Between the stone piers the sea was foaming and an immense shape reared from the scattering fog.

It was impossible to see what manner of living thing it was. It looked like an island risen from uncharted depths. Enormous shells and clumps of coral encrusted its craggy surface. On its highest ridge they formed a steepled tower. It sailed up the Esk with slow and stately majesty, stopping just before the bridge. The seals barked a welcome and a din like many horns blowing sounded from the crustaceans. The greatest shells in that tower uncurled and a sea bishop waggled forward, moving with stiff dignity and grandeur until it reached the nearest point to the bridge where it stared at the marquess and his brides to be.

It was a hideous, ancient creature. Smaller than an aufwader, it was covered in tough skin and carapace. The face was flat and the eyes were dark slits above a wide, downturned mouth. The limbs were spindly and the inflexible hide made movement almost impossible.

The flat face angled round to take in the prospect of the expectant town. The aufwaders were on their knees and the humans were glassy eyed and staring. The sea bishop made a repellent gurgling. But everyone understood what it said. They heard its high, arrogant voice inside their heads.

'Mister Dark, I am come to preside over your briding. You must appreciate how highly the Lords of the Deep favour you in this.'

'I'm extremely honoured, your grace,' the man answered. 'But my name now is the Marquess Darqueller, if you please.'

'You are Mister Dark and that is how I shall address you and how you must name yourself in this ceremony, or it will not be binding.'

'As your grace wishes. It must be binding.'

'Which of those females is to be the bride?'

'All three of them, your grace.'

'Is that usual in a human union?'

'What does that matter?'

'So be it. Let the briding commence.'

'I have Their blessing then?'

'I would not be here if you did not!'

The marquess grinned and took out the red lacquer box.

'I have here the blood dowries!' he called. 'Under cover of stars and moon do I, Mister Dark, pledge mine intent – to make for mine own Grace Pickering, Martha Gales and Princess Maud, and bestow upon them such gifts that are in my power, that they shall obey me in all things.'

'Here's for the Lord of the Circling Seas,' he proclaimed, emptying the blood from each phial into the river. 'Here's for the Lord of the Roaring Waters. And here's for the Lord of the Frozen Wastes.'

Where the blood fell, three scarlet streams formed in the river, widening and merging until the whole harbour was filled with blood.

'Are the dowries accepted?' the marquess asked.

'They are, as you can see.'

'Now is the bond made and I call upon the sea itself, and you, your grace, to witness it.'

'By the Three powers vested in me, from the Dark Realm, I pronounce this briding bound and true. None may cleave you asunder. So shall it be, thrice over.'

'So shall it be,' the marquess repeated with a note of triumph in his voice. 'Thrice over.'

The sea bishop turned, the creatures of the sea made a jubilant clamour, the whales blew spouts of blood into the air and the sea birds screeched a deafening riot.

The marquess turned to Verne. 'Now, boy,' he commanded.

Verne held up the Nimius and clicked one of the symbols. The topmost section rose up and the jewel beneath shone out.

'What is this?' the sea bishop demanded. 'This is not part of the briding.'

'Oh, it is, your grace,' the marquess said, not bothering to mask his scorn any longer. 'Blood is the bridge and you have accepted all three on behalf of Them.'

The sea bishop tottered backwards in horror. 'You dare do this?' it cried.

'Oh, I dare, yes, and the power of the Nimius gives me the strength to enforce it.'

At that moment the sea shook and the cliffs of Whitby trembled. Instead of pealing, the bells began to toll. On the East Pier the aufwaders cried out. Abel pulled Nettie, Hesper and his father back on to the Scaur, towards the doors to the caves. The other fisherfolk followed in a panic.

'Vain, petty man!' the sea bishop denounced him. 'That device is not enough to overthrow Them. Hear and see how you have squandered Their favour and earned Their unending wrath for this folly . . .'

'Yes, I know the Nimius is not powerful enough,' yelled Mister Dark, but he was laughing. 'Why do you think I journeyed back to a time when the Nimius was still buried and hidden on the cliff? Don't you see, you ugly imbecile, there are two in existence here now and I'm going to awaken the other.'

He clicked his fingers. Verne twisted a scrolling lever. The projecting crystal throbbed with emerald light. Over on the East Cliff an answering shaft of green burst from the soil.

'No!' the sea bishop shrieked as it realised the horrendous truth. 'You are mad! Mad!'

'Oh, no!' crowed Dark. 'Not mad. I am Their husband! The bond was accepted, the bridge was made and the Lords of the Deep are now my brides! Come, my vast, immortal loves, obey your new master. The ceremony commands it and I have the power to compel you!'

Grasping Grace's shoulders he shouted at the angry waves that came surging up the harbour mouth. 'Lord of the Circling Seas, I give you the gift of this body to inhabit. Blood is the bridge, so shall it be!'

The Nimius in Verne's hands quaked and the emerald light intensified. The other source on the cliff did the same. There was no power on earth to withstand their combined might.

In the entrance to their tunnels, heaving frantically on the ancient mechanism to close the rocky doors, the aufwaders stared out to sea in horror. A forest of lighting blazed on the horizon. From the deepest regions, one of the omnipotent rulers of the world was forced to obey the Marquess Darqueller. The Lord of the Circling Seas reared in the distance and Nettie hid her face in Hesper's shoulder. Tarr staggered against his son and Abel yelled for the doors to close. The chains rattled and the great cogs turned. The doors slammed shut and the terror stricken aufwaders fled into the deepest caves.

On the bridge, the body of Grace sagged. Euphoric, the marquess watched as her face divided and split into segments that grew into serpent-like tentacles that ripped through the veil and spilled from her sleeves.

'Lord of the Roaring Waters!' he exulted next. 'I give you the gift of Martha Gales's body to inhabit. Blood is the bridge, so shall it be!'

The thunder grew louder as another titan of the world was dragged from the cold fastness of the Dark Realm. The bellowing rage blasted around the globe, but there was no withstanding the pull of the Nimii. And so the eternal, immeasurable mind of the Lord of the Roaring Waters was siphoned down into the head of a dead girl's corpse.

At the Union Mill, Bram Stoker had rushed out after the coach and watched it dash towards the harbour. Mastering his repulsion at the sight of Mrs Axmill's body, he removed the gun from her hand and tucked it into his belt. Then he ran to the side of the building where the unloaded wagons stood.

Inside the mill, Nannie was systematically smashing the tanks with her poker, putting any creature that came crawling from them out of its misery with one merciful blow.

Irving had inspected the dials on a bank of controls and was twisting every valve until the needles veered sharply into the red and the noise of the generators escalated to shrill whines. Blistering steam erupted from the pipes and he hoped the sabotage would be enough.

'*Come, let us take a muster speedily!*' he urged Nannie and Lil. '*Doomsday is near!*'

Lil didn't seem to hear him. She was staring at the slab where Verne had lain. There was nothing more she could do. Why had she ever hoped she could rescue Verne? Who was she to challenge an agent of the Deep Ones? She was only a frightened child. A child who had stretched her neck out too far, daring to interfere in matters far beyond her understanding. And now it was over.

Around her, flames burst from the machines and arcs of static flashed from one wall to another. A rending and clanging of metal announced the collapse of a tower of copper tubing, which ripped down a web of cables in its ruin. Sparks exploded in every direction.

Then, in the midst of that chaos and destruction, Lil's outer senses closed down. Her world became dark and silent. But there was a shape in the darkness. It was the ruined abbey and, standing in one of the windows, was a shining figure. A woman's voice called to her across a vast distance, but she couldn't make out the words.

'Miss Lil!' Henry Irving cried, putting his arm around her and wrenching her away from the slab where embers were raining from above. 'We must abandon this cloud-clapp'd tower.'

With Nannie's help, he guided her through the burning mill, dodging around the scalding steam, halting only when they were outside.

The mill was burning furiously. The sails were cloaked in flame and it was crowned with lightning.

'Here's two carthorses,' Stoker called to them. 'They'll get us down to the harbour faster than Shanks's pony. Nannie, get on behind me. Lil, you're with Irving.'

Soon they were cantering down the streets and Nannie was clinging to Mr Stoker with her eyes shut and her skirts flying, whirling the poker over her head. Lil was still in a daze. When she saw the abbey on the far cliff, she stared at it, willing the shining figure to reappear.

They arrived at the quayside just as the bells began to toll.

A great crowd of bewitched townsfolk stood between them and the bridge, where the marquess was taunting the sea bishop and telling Verne to awaken the other Nimius.

As the second green light blazed through the darkness, up on the East Cliff, Lil continued to stare at the abbey. Again she heard a voice.

'Why?' she murmured. 'I don't understand . . . tell me.'

'What in the nine rings of hell is going on?' Stoker demanded, staring at the two emerald beacons. 'What's the lad think he's doing there? What's that weird scrap of a being our filthy marquess is talking to and what's the putrid island it's stood on?'

A thundering tempest out at sea drew everyone's attention and he, Irving and Nannie witnessed the Lord of the Circling Seas rupturing the stormy waves.

'My God!' Irving uttered.

'One of them,' Nannie agreed. Sliding off the carthorse she pushed her way to the front of the crowd and looked in dread at the nightmare on the horizon.

Dragging her eyes from the abbey, Lil rubbed her forehead. Hastily collecting her thoughts, she stared over at Verne and the secondary pinnacle of green light, and understood at once what was happening.

'He's doubled the Nimius's power.' she cried.

'That gold gadget from the mill?' Stoker asked. 'Is that what's causing this lunacy?'

Lil nodded. 'There's nothing anyone can do,' she said.

'Is there not?' the Irishman replied, taking the gun from his belt and steadying it on his forearm as he took aim.

'A bullet won't kill Mister Dark,' Lil told him. 'You're wasting your time.'

'I'm not aiming at him, miss. I'm awful sorry, but I've got to shoot your friend there. He's the one operating that mad engine of destruction.'

'Verne?' Lil shrieked. 'No!'

'It's the only way. Might be the kindest act anyway, after what that monster's done to him.'

Lil leapt from her horse and reached up to pull Stoker down from his. He kicked her aside, calling for Irving to restrain her. The actor jumped down behind and seized Lil's arms, dragging her away.

'It's for the good of all!' he told her. 'You must see this! It's deplorable, but it's the only way.'

'No,' Lil said, angrily. 'I don't care about anything else. Just Verne.'

Kicking Irving in the shin, she tore herself free. The crowd had closed in around Stoker's horse, blocking her way. The bridge was closer. Lil barged through.

Martha Gales's body had become a thrashing pillar of slime and snaking arms, and they writhed and churned in the wedding gown. She and the nightmare Grace had become were a nauseating sight.

'What gorgeous wives I have!' the marquess yelled. 'Now, my loves, obey your husband, as is your lot in

our new connubial state. Demonstrate to me what clever helpmeets you are.'

He cast around and pointed out to sea. 'Raise a ridge of mountains, just there,' he said. 'You must do as I command. I am your husband and master.'

The fearsome brides raised their flailing arms. The North Yorkshire coast shook and the waters parted. Pinnacles of black rock came rearing from the sea, forming an impassable wall beyond the harbour.

'Higher, higher,' he ordered. 'Dwarf the abbey, that's right. Now stop. What next?'

He thought for a moment then sniggered capriciously. 'Ah, yes. Sink France. All of it. I don't like the French. I was insulted there once.'

The continents shuddered as they ripped apart and the entire land mass of France went crashing into an abyss. The tremors tore across Europe and tsunamis devastated the neighbouring countries. Chaos and catastrophe travelled round the globe. Only Whitby was safe.

The marquess laughed louder. Then he looked down at the Princess Maud, propped against the rail. She was still drugged.

'Time for my third bride to don this new flesh,' he said, lifting her. Before he called on the Lord of the Frozen Wastes, he gazed on the royal neck.

'Such a sacrifice these girls have been for me, surrendering their bodies to their new owners, but this one most of all, the finest neck I have ever seen.' Stooping over her, he kissed it.

Stoker was waiting for a clear shot at Verne. When the ground was shaking and the mountain peaks appeared, it was impossible. His horse stamped and shied. But Irving had calmed it and held the beast's head steady. Now . . . yes, Bram saw a great chance, right through the boy's chest.

'Do it,' Irving urged. 'That's Her Majesty's granddaughter down there, being slobbered over by that devil. Shoot the boy! End this woe and destruction!'

'Aye,' Stoker said, half closing an eye. He moistened his bottom lip and took a steadying breath. His finger squeezed the trigger.

The bullet fired harmlessly into the air.

'What happened?' Irving cried.

'I've got a ten-year-old lad myself,' Bram answered grimly. 'And not just that – I'm not a one for killing kids and if you think I could our partnership is ended.'

Irving glared at him, then rested his head against the horse's neck. 'You're right, my friend,' he said. 'We must not become monsters ourselves.'

Hearing the shot, Lil stared anxiously at Verne. When she saw he was unharmed, she pushed the remaining people out of her way and ran to him.

'Don't do this!' she pleaded. 'Switch the Nimius off. Smash it – anything.'

'I can't. Mister Dark is too strong. I have to do what he says.'

'Listen to me, Verne Thistlewood. I know you're stronger.'

'I'm Flimsy, remember? You're the strong one.'

'That's not true! We're strongest when we're together and I'm never going to leave you again. Do you hear me?'

'He'll kill us both.'

The girl glanced up at the East Cliff.

'I don't think so,' she said. 'Now switch off the one hidden up there and send this one home. Then there'll only be one here.'

'And us go with it?'

'No.'

'Why?'

'Just do it.'

'Lord of the Frozen Wastes!' the marquess shouted. 'I give you the gift of Princess Maud's body to inhabit. Blood is the br–'

He faltered. The emerald light on the cliff was flickering and dying.

He spun round in time to see Verne pushing a sequence of symbols and turning a dial. The Nimius lifted from his hands and revolved in mid-air. The green light was extinguished and the golden device became wreathed in purple flames.

'No!' the marquess bawled. 'I'll kill you, boy!'

The Nimius whirled faster. Then it was gone.

The marquess screamed with rage. Then he realised his peril. He had no protection now. He had tried to enslave the Lords of the Deep and Dark by making them his brides and there was no escaping their rage.

The harrowing creatures in the wedding gowns turned and slithered towards him.

'All right!' he snarled. 'So this is how Mister Dark ends. But he had a grand ride of it. And it's not over yet, because I'll not go down on my own.'

He leaped at Verne and Lil, determined to drag them into those reaching tentacles. But Verne wrapped his arms around Lil, gave a tremendous thrust with his wings and they soared over the river.

The marquess screeched at them. Then a poker smashed against his shoulder and another blow hammered upon his knee. Nannie Burdon stood before him, her face set and ready to deliver another thrashing. Yowling a battle cry, she forced him backwards, into the waiting clutches of his brides. A clammy coil whipped around his throat, throttling his screams, and they pulled him into their embrace. The wedding dresses seethed with fury and the supernatural life the Lords of the Deep had granted to him was taken away.

Nannie watched with satisfaction.

'Drink deep this bottler's curse, Mister Dark,' she said grimly. 'May your evil never arise. Go back to being a bad memory, a bedtime bogeyman to scare the kiddies. Tread not this shore again.'

When they were done, the brides cast Mister Dark's crushed body into the river. The surface boiled as every creature surged to feed on him, even the gulls swooped to rip and rend. The hideous forms in the wedding gowns retreated, departing those temporary hosts. The vast minds of the Deep Ones were free and they returned to their true forms, submerging back to the Dark Realm.

On the bridge the two dead girls fell to the ground. Nannie knelt by them and stroked their fair faces.

Irving and Stoker rode up on the horses. Bram lifted the unconscious Princess Maud and sat her in front of him. Nannie Burdon rose and turned to regard the sea bishop. She bowed, then rested her arms on the rail and addressed it.

'You came this close today, your grace.'

'Indeed I know,' it said. 'What would you have me do in gratitude?'

'Oh, you know the answer to that,' she said, beaming at him. 'That's what I'm here for. I'm the Whitby witch. Repair what he did, let the locals sleep it off and forget, the usual palaver.'

'Now that sounds like something I could put my name down for,' Irving said, wiping his brow. 'I've no wish to be tormented by this the rest of my life. How about you, Stoker?'

The Irishman sucked his teeth as he considered. 'You might be tempted, but I'll not surrender memories so dearly bought, no matter how horrific.'

The actor gave a weary groan. 'So be it,' he said. 'Just promise you won't scribble about any of this. Your florid prose is dreadful.'

Nannie looked once more at Grace and Martha.

'What about these two poor lasses here?' she asked the sea bishop. 'Is there a chance of bringing them back? I know nothing is beyond the power of the Three.'

'The flesh in which They were almost imprisoned must remain dead,' it told her firmly. 'Do not ask again! Your other requests . . . I am empowered to negotiate.'

Nannie rested her chin on her hands. 'I warn you, sunshine,' she said with a gleam in her eye. 'I'm a little belter of a haggler.'

FUR AND FEATHERS

With Lil in his arms, Verne glided high over Whitby. Flying using the Nimius wasn't the same as beating your own wings and riding the updrafts. This was fantastic. But he was too weak to carry his friend far, so he headed to the graveyard. As he descended, a dark shape dived on to his back and Catesby began slashing the membranes of his wings, tearing them with his claws and ripping them with his teeth.

Verne and Lil plummeted. Catesby hissed and pursued them.

'Hey, Frankenpuss!' a voice called out. 'Get an eyeful of this technicolor tushy!'

A clash of bright colours slammed into Catesby. Still possessed by Cherry Cerise, George the parrot battled the creature in a bitter, vicious duel in the sky.

Lil and Verne crashlanded on the grassy slope at the edge of the graveyard. Lil was winded but unharmed. She knelt at Verne's side. He was unconscious and his wings were in tatters.

Hearing the desperate fight above, Lil watched George and Catesby reel through the air, wings flapping feverishly. Claws raking, fangs snapping and beak biting, they slammed against the church tower then disappeared over the cliff edge, only to rise up again still brawling. Bright feathers and clumps of fur drizzled down.

As they fought, one of the parrot's feet clutched tight to Catesby's neck and his beak went scraping against the skull.

'How about some air con in that ugly head of yours?' Cherry said as the beak clamped on to a metal staple and prised it free.

Catesby screeched. Then another staple was torn out, and another.

The skull fell apart, and George's other foot went for a paddle inside.

Mister Dark's familiar went limp and the parrot let him fall. He smashed on to the rocks of the Scaur and the sea dragged him away.

'So,' Cherry said, as the parrot landed on the nearest headstone to Lil and Verne. 'You do know you're stuck here, right? You sent the Nimius hightailing forward to the future on its own. Whose dumb cluck idea was that?'

'Mine,' Lil said.

'Major fail. Wanna try running that past me?'

Lil glanced beyond the church to the ruins of the abbey.

'I was told to,' she said.

'What jackass told you that?'

'I'm not sure,' Lil answered uncertainly. 'It was a voice. It said there was still something left to do here.'

'Sure, develop rickets and live through a world war – two, if you last that long.'

At Lil's feet, Verne was coming round. The girl stooped to stroke his hair. The sun was coming up and the grass was drenched in dew.

'The voice called a name as well,' she told Cherry. 'It was really insistent.'

'What name?'

Lil put her friend's head in her lap

'Don't you worry, Verne,' she said. 'We'll get through this. We're together now. You and me are unstoppable.'

'What name?' Cherry repeated.

Lil looked into the parrot's bright blue eyes.

'Alice Boston,' she said.

Don't miss

LEGACY
OF
WITCHES

Coming soon